PAUL STEWART

Rory McCrory's Nightmare Machine

Illustrated by Paul Finn

VIKING

By the same author

ADAM'S ARK
THE THOUGHT DOMAIN
THE WEATHER WITCH

For Julie and Joseph

VIKING

Published by the Penguin Group
Penguin Books Ltd, 27 Wrights Lane, London W8 5TZ, England
Penguin Books USA Inc., 375 Hudson Street, New York, New York 10014, USA
Penguin Books Australia Ltd, Ringwood, Victoria, Australia
Penguin Books Canada Ltd, 10 Alcorn Avenue, Toronto, Ontario, Canada M4V 3B2
Penguin Books (NZ) Ltd, 182–190 Wairau Road, Auckland 10, New Zealand

Penguin Books Ltd, Registered Offices: Harmondsworth, Middlesex, England

First published 1992
1 3 5 7 9 10 8 6 4 2

Text copyright © Paul Stewart, 1992
Illustrations copyright © Paul Finn, 1992

The moral right of the author has been asserted

Filmset in Palatino
Printed in England by Clays Ltd, St Ives plc

A CIP catalogue record for this book is available from the British Library

ISBN 0–670–84127–7

THURSDAY THE FOURTEENTH OF SEPTEMBER AT SEVEN O'CLOCK IN THE HALL AT PORTREE. SHALL COMMENCE A PERFORMANCE *OF*

Rory McCrory's

Real~to~Reel
~Picture Show~

Do Come. It'll Change your life! See you there. R. McC

(ADMISSION REFUSED TO PERSONS OVER THE AGE OF 14)

—1—

AN ACT OF DEFIANCE

'Look!' yelled Fiona, jumping up and pointing out to sea.

'What?' Alex asked. He squinted at the bright, choppy waves, trying to see what his sister had spotted.

'Over there,' she said. 'It keeps disappearing behind the . . . THERE! Can you see it?'

Alex nodded. 'Do you think there's a message in it?'

'Only one way to find out,' said Fiona. 'One of us will have to go in.'

'I'll toss you for it,' Alex said, pulling out a coin from his pocket.

'Heads.'

'Blast!' he muttered. 'Heads it is.'

Jamie remained glumly silent while Alex stripped down to his underpants and began wading out into the cold, grey water. He was relieved that his friends were sensitive enough not to ask him if he'd be prepared to retrieve the bottle, but all the same, it made him both angry and miserable that his dread of water left him excluded from so

3

simple a task. Hydrophobia was the last thing you needed when you lived on an island — not that he was afraid of *all* water: he didn't have rabies. No, drinking the stuff was fine, but the wild turbulence of a river or the swell of the sea was something else. Just the thought of being overcome by its merciless grip was enough to fill him with numbing horror.

'It's f — f — freezing,' Alex stuttered as the water reached his waist. He kicked off towards the object bobbing in and out of sight ahead of him.

'He's nearly got it,' Fiona shouted at Jamie. 'Come and have a look.'

Jamie felt uneasy, and it wasn't only because of the water. Mention of the bottle had triggered off half-forgotten associations in his memory. Obediently, he walked over to Fiona, but the dragged footprints in the gravelly sand bore witness to his reluctance.

'He's got it,' Fiona was saying. 'Come on!' she called to her brother.

'All . . . ight,' came the staccato reply, as his words were whipped away on the blustery wind. With the bottle in his left hand, Alex side-stroked back to the beach as fast as he could. The cross-current was treacherous and after several minutes of strenuous kicking, he finally came ashore some fifty metres further along the beach.

'Let's see,' said Fiona, grabbing at her brother's hand.

'Hang on, hang on,' Alex shivered. 'Who went and got it?'

'Well, hurry up,' Fiona said, as Alex dried himself on his vest as best he could.

The deep-green glass was so dark that it was impossible to see whether the discarded wine bottle had anything in it. The suspense became intolerable as Alex took forever putting his clothes back on and tying his shoe-laces just the way he liked them.

'Come *on*!' Fiona protested.

'There's probably nothing in it anyway,' said Jamie.

'Course there is,' she said. 'Why else would someone put the cork back in?'

Dressed at last, Alex lifted the bottle up to the sky and peered at it intently. Unless it was a trick of the light, the silhouette looked promising. He popped the cork out and poked down inside the neck.

'Turn it upside down and bang it,' Fiona instructed excitedly.

'I think I've . . .' Alex said as his finger brushed the edge of a coiled piece of card. 'If I can just –'

'Oh, smash the bottle,' said Fiona, impatient as always.

'No, don't,' Jamie insisted.

'Why not?' Fiona demanded.

'It's bad luck.'

'Who says?'

'I read it somewhere,' he muttered sullenly.

'It's OK,' said Alex. 'Here it comes.'

Stained with pink blots of the wine dregs, the tube of card was about fifteen centimetres wide and, when unrolled, ten centimetres long.

'What is it?' Fiona asked.

'Thursday, the fourteenth of September,' Alex read from the ornate announcement, 'at seven o'clock in the Hall at Portree shall commence a performance of *Rory McCrory's Real-to-Reel Picture Show*. (Admission refused to persons over the age of 14.) And then there's a picture of an old projector and . . .'

'Is that all?' Fiona said.

Everyone on the island already knew about the imminent arrival of the travelling cinema. Posters advertising the event had gone up weeks earlier, and even though Fiona was looking forward to the show itself, it was disappointing that the bottle had merely contained a reminder.

'*And,*' Alex continued, 'there's something else at the bottom — it's not printed like the rest.'

Fiona craned her neck to see. There, in navy-blue italics, was a personal message from Rory McCrory himself.

'*Do come. It'll change your life! See you there*. R. McC.'

'Change your life!' Fiona snorted. 'As if!'

Alex laughed. His sister was nothing if not down-to-earth. Astrology, magic, omens and superstitions: they were nothing but old wives' tales to Fiona. She was far too practical to believe in anything she couldn't taste, touch, hear, see, smell — or spend. Jamie — an Aquarius — was quite the opposite. He would walk round ladders, touch wood, and throw spilt salt over his shoulder. He would always count the number of magpies he saw to determine whether good or bad luck would follow and, if it was bad, he would spend hours searching for a four-leaved clover to counter the inevitable ill-fortune.

When Alex had read out Rory McCrory's remarkable promise, icy fingers of terror had strummed the length of Jamie's spine. He looked away, anxious not to let the others see his obvious panic.

'I'd better be going,' he said. 'Shouldn't be late.'

Fiona and Alex made no comment. They knew only too well how bad-tempered his father could be. Mr MacDonald was renowned throughout the island for his harshness — it was rumoured that, for the most trivial of misdemeanours, he would beat his son with a heavy belt. The rumours were unfounded, and yet the man's sharp, sarcastic tongue caused Jamie more pain than could any strip of leather.

'Are you coming to the picture show tonight?' Fiona shouted after him.

'Have to see,' he called back without turning round.

'Which means no,' Fiona muttered to her brother. 'He's never allowed to do *anything*.'

6

'Poor Jamie,' Alex nodded. 'If anyone's life needs changing, it's his.'

The boy cut a pathetic figure as he crossed the beach, diagonally, up towards the town. The awkward scrawniness of his body was exaggerated by the size of the blazer, which his mother had assured him he would 'grow into.' When? That was the question. The sleeves that she would carefully fold back each morning had slipped back down over his hands, so that only the tips of his fingers were showing. Thin, bony legs protruded from his baggy shorts: he was the only boy in his year not yet in long trousers.

Over the years, shoulder-length hair, crew-cuts and flat-tops had all passed him by. His father insisted that he always ask for short back and sides and, despite promising himself that 'next time' he would ask for what *he* wanted, at twelve years old Jamie had still never dared to. Instead, after each visit to the barber's, he'd had to endure the taunts and stinging slaps of fourth-form rulers on the exposed white skin at the back of his neck. Until recently, that is.

London teenagers had revived the old-fashioned haircut and four months earlier, Keith Dalmally – who was in the fifth year, drove a Honda 50 and played bass guitar in a local band called Forked Tongue – had brought the style to Portree High. Before the summer term was over, most of the boys were sporting the same cut. For the first time in his life, Jamie found himself in the middle of a trend. Knowing his father, he would probably now insist that he let his hair grow over his ears.

'Is that you, dear?' he heard as he opened the back door and kicked off his shoes on the kitchen mat. His mother asked the same question every day, in the same tone of voice, at the same volume, her reedy voice rising on the 'you'. Today was just the same as every other day.

'No, Jack the Ripper,' he muttered. He had planned to

tape her voice each afternoon for a fortnight, and then play the questions back, one after the other. 'Is that you, dear? Is that you, dear? Is that you . . .' Over and over the words would repeat like a scratched record.

'Ja-mie?'

The follow-up question; his name quavering to a crescendo on the 'mie'.

'Yes, Mum, it's me,' he said.

Mrs MacDonald was sitting on the sofa, knitting. She was always knitting. She loved watching the strip of woven wool growing in size until it spilled over her lap; she loved the regular click of the needles beating time with the mantelpiece clock; she loved the way her fingers scurried about their business without any conscious effort, while she listened to the radio, or simply drifted off into her memories. But while loving the knitting itself, Mrs MacDonald hated finishing anything off. She was perpetually surrounded by mounds of sleeves, fronts and backs, all waiting to be stitched together.

Her reluctance to finish the job was in all likelihood to avoid disappointment. The end result never lived up to her expectations; never looked like the photograph on the front of the pattern. The sweaters were shapeless, the cardigans massive, and even an elephant would not have been able to keep Mrs MacDonald's socks up.

'How was school, dear?' she asked, glancing up at her son.

'All right.'

She returned to her knitting. ''S coming along,' she added a moment later, and waved the huge, woollen expanse of beige at him.

Jamie smiled weakly. From the pieces she'd already held up against him, he knew that this sleeveless pullover would be as shapeless as all the rest: too short, too baggy, and so wide at the neck it would slip down over his shoulder.

'Any homework?'

'A bit. I'll get it done now.'

His dad arrived home at six. It was best to have it out of the way by then – in the past, Jamie's homework had led to far too many rows. His handwriting wouldn't be neat enough, the maps he drew too inaccurate, the arithmetic would use methods Mr MacDonald couldn't understand.

'Not like in my day,' he'd say. 'We respected our masters and we learnt things properly.

> *I met a traveller from an antique land*
> *Who said: The vast and trunkless legs of stone*
> *Stand in the desert . . . Near them, on the sand,*
> *Half sunk, a shattered visage lies, whose frown,*
> *And wrinkled lip, and sneer of cold command,*
> *Tell that its sculptor will . . . well . . . will. . .*

Will or well? I met a traveller . . .' He raced through the poem again up to the point where he'd got stuck.

'. . . WELL those passions read . . .'

He had turned triumphantly towards his son. '*That's* learning,' he'd said. 'Forty-one years ago I was told to memorize it, and memorize it I did. You'd get the strap if so much as one word was wrong.'

Jamie had read *Ozymandias* in English, and the class had talked about the arrogance of great men who build memorials, monuments and mausoleums to themselves, in the vain hope that they might somehow achieve immortality. But everyone dies and everything – even marble and bronze – crumbles away one day. Jamie had looked at his father. From the way he'd read the poem, stopping at the end of each line, it was clear that the man hadn't understood a single word. No, Jamie couldn't parrot the work, but there was no doubt which of the two had got more from Shelley's masterpiece.

There was no English homework tonight though. A bit of arithmetic and some history. Jamie hated numbers, but finding the highest common multiple was easy enough if you followed the formula, and he finished it off in under ten minutes. The history assignment was altogether more interesting.

He had to pretend he was one of the citizens of Paris in 1789 and write an account of the Revolution through his or her eyes. Jamie had thought of being a poor farmer who had come to the city in search of work, but the sight of his mother on the sofa had changed his mind. He would be one of the *tricoteuses*: the old women who had sat in the front row at the executions, knitting away furiously while the aristocrats were guillotined, one after the other.

'Tea's on the table,' his mother's voice announced, what seemed like a moment later. Homework was easy when you enjoyed it.

'Just coming.'

Already six o'clock, Jamie realized. His dad would be home. Hopefully he'd be in a good mood. It wasn't very likely that he'd let Jamie go to the picture show anyway, but if he'd had a bad day at the office, it wouldn't even be worth asking. He reread his gory and gleeful account of Marie Antoinette's head dropping into the basket.

Not bad at all, he thought, and stuffed the exercise books back into his satchel.

'Evening, Dad,' he said cheerfully.

His father merely grunted. It was not looking promising. The pair of them sat in grim silence throughout the liver and bacon. As usual, Mrs MacDonald remained on the sofa, knitting. 'I'll get myself a bite to eat later,' she would inevitably say, and interrupt her latest woolly creation only to serve up the dessert.

At a quarter past six Jamie knew that if he was going to make the start of Rory McCrory's picture show, he would have to ask soon. But his father still looked so grumpy. Half-way through the jam roly-poly and custard, he could keep quiet no longer.

'Dad,' he said.

No response.

'Dad, the travelling cinema's on tonight. It's the last visit to the island this year. Can I go, please? Everyone else is going,' he added, hoping that this might sway the decision.

'Why do you always have to copy everyone else?' Mr MacDonald said, without looking up.

Jamie sighed. He really couldn't win. The previous week he'd asked for a pair of shoes with buckles, stressing the fact that no one else had any. 'Why do you always have to be different?' his father had immediately snapped back. Jamie hadn't got the shoes he'd wanted and it was looking increasingly unlikely that he'd be allowed to the cinema show either.

He looked at his mother for support, but she kept her head down, concentrating on the knitting.

Mr MacDonald laid his spoon down and patted his lips with his napkin.

'Have you done your homework?' he asked.

'Yes,' said Jamie, sensing a possible shift of mood. 'Arithmetic and history.'

'Let me see it. If I think it's good enough, you can go.'

Jamie fetched his books reluctantly. 'If I think it's good enough' was tantamount to saying no.

'What is this anyway?' he asked, looking at Jamie's neat calculations.

'Highest common multiple,' he said.

'Not like *proper* arithmetic,' he said scornfully. 'Not like we had in my day.'

'It's quite hard to do.'

'Evidently. This is wrong for a start.'

'No, you don't know how to do it,' Jamie protested.

'What are five twenty-twos?'

Jamie tried to work the sum out in his head, but it was hopeless. The numbers wouldn't stay in the right place, and he kept forgetting the figures he'd carried over. He felt himself redden with tingling frustration.

'I'll have to write it down and . . .'

'It's easy,' his father said dismissively. 'Five twenties are a hundred. Five twos are ten. A hundred and ten.'

Jamie heard the words, but couldn't follow the reasoning. It wasn't the way he'd been taught to multiply. It was all right for his father: as an accountant, he was used to playing around with figures all day.

'Careless,' his father announced, as he tossed the book on to the table. 'And what else have you done?'

Jamie handed him the history exercise book, and sat back nervously in his chair while his father read through the account of Marie Duvall. He watched the man's thick eyebrows rise with surprise, then frown ominously.

And I don't care that she has got the same name as me, I'm glad the Austrian mair is going to lose her head. She never had to scrimp and save to provide a decent meal for her hungry children. She never had to trapse from town to town searching for a job.

She's up on the wooden podium now. She's begging for mercy. Not likely. Hailstones destroy the wheat harvest two years on the run, and she tells us to eat cakes! Good riddance to bad rubbish I say. Her head is on the block. The guillotine is swishing down.

Whoops, nearly dropped a stitch.

'How do you spell *mare*?'

'M-a-i-r.'

'R-e, r-e,' Mr MacDonald yelled. 'Don't they teach you anything at school? And traipse?'

'Spelling's not so important any more,' Jamie mumbled miserably. He'd never get to the cinema show now.

12

'Not important? How do they expect you to get a job afterwards, turning out illiterates? And what's this meant to be anyway? History? Where are the dates? Where are the facts?'

'But . . .'

'And why are you pretending to be a woman? What's the matter with you? Eh? If you must write this sort of drivel, why can't you at least be a man?'

He sneered and turned away. Jamie felt his heart racing, his stomach churning, his scalp prickling. Why couldn't the man simply vanish? Disappear? If he hated everything so much, why didn't he just go away?

But that would never happen. Jamie breathed in deeply and tried to stop his voice from cracking.

'So, can I go?' he asked.

'Yes,' said his father.

'I can?' Jamie said, hardly able to believe his luck.

'You can go to your room. I don't want to see you till the morning.'

'But, Dad . . .'

'NOW,' his father bellowed.

As he left the room, Jamie glanced over at his mother. She had continued knitting throughout the entire episode, her needles missing not a single beat.

Yes, Jamie thought bitterly, you'd have made a brilliant *tricoteuse*.

The street-lamps were already on outside; it would soon be winter. Jamie looked through his window at the blustery evening. He imagined all his classmates leaving their houses and making for the Church Hall, where the performance of the travelling cinema was due to take place. Everyone except him. Tears welled up in his eyes and, as he tried to stop himself crying, the lump in his throat ached. He swallowed.

'It isn't fair,' he mumbled miserably, his breath misting up the glass. No one else's father could possible be so mean, and he found himself tracing letters in the patch of condensation.

BIG SMELLY BULLY.

He looked round the all-too familiar room. His father always insisted that he go to bed at eight, even though he was never the slightest bit tired then. He claimed it was for the boy's own good; that he needed his sleep. But Jamie knew it was because his father wanted him out of the way in the evenings. He would sit at the window staring outside, recording in his diary the neighbourhood comings and goings. The exercise book was one long list of minute trivia. This evening was to prove no different.

'18 minutes to 7: next-door's dog passed by. 14 minutes to 7: John Girvan and Liam Donahue walked past, eating chips from the paper.'

Probably on their way to the picture show, Jamie noted dejectedly.

'12 minutes to 7: next-door's dog returned.'

The angry words on the window that he could never say to his father were fading away. He knew that if he went to bed now, sleep would be full of hideous nightmares: it was always the same when they'd been arguing. All the things he wanted to say and all the feelings he was forced to suppress would come bubbling up to the surface the moment he drifted off, to torment him through the night. He would dream he was sobbing inconsolably and wake up with red eyes and a damp pillow.

The message in the bottle came back to him. *Do come. It'll change your life! See you there.* And signed by Rory McCrory himself.

See you there!

Yes, he would see him. He *would*. Jamie was suddenly convinced that the message was intended specifically for him. The travelling-cinema man must have known all about Jamie MacDonald and sent the bottle to reassure him. *It'll change your life!* How could he miss such an opportunity.

'I *am* going,' Jamie murmured, shocked, but encouraged by the words he had uttered.

Saying it was one thing, however, doing it was another. The MacDonalds lived in a bungalow, so there would be no problem with the jump down, but Jamie's bedroom window consisted of an unopenable pane of glass with a narrow hinged affair above it. It was far too small for him to squeeze through. He was trapped.

The room opposite his had proper windows — they had remained unchanged when the rest of the house was double-glazed — but Jamie hated going in there. It contained too many disturbing memories. But this was no time for squeamishness. Only ten minutes remained before the start of the performance.

He hurriedly stuffed his pillow under the blankets and, satisfied that the lump could pass for a sleeping boy, eased open his bedroom door. Muffled sounds of canned laughter emanated sporadically from the television, and Jamie pictured the sitting-room scene: father in armchair cradling a glass of malt whisky; mother on settee, knitting.

It's just not fair, he reminded himself.

He tiptoed across the carpet to the closed door. As far back as he could remember, it had always been kept shut. There was a click as he turned the door handle. The noise seemed to echo the length of the hall and Jamie froze. He heard the unfamiliar sound of his father laughing at the sitcom, and held his breath as he went in, praying that the unused hinges wouldn't squeak. He was in luck. So far, so good.

Resting for a moment, he leant back against the door and

tried to stop his heart pumping quite so furiously. As his eyes became accustomed to the eerie gloom created by the sodium lamps outside, he looked around.

It was quite clearly a girl's room. There was make-up on the dressing-table; dolls, teddies, clowns and an assortment of furry animals lining the bed, propped up against the wall; posters of pop stars were Blu-tacked to the multi-coloured geometric wallpaper.

Jamie remembered how he had once followed his father into the room while his mother was cleaning. Mr Mac-Donald had started on about one of the men on the walls.

'I mean what does he look like? Lipstick and plaits — like some lass. Pervert, that's what he is. A per-vert,' he had repeated, spitting out the words contemptuously.

'She liked him,' his mother had answered simply.

'And look where it got her, I —'

Mr MacDonald noticed Jamie standing in the doorway and held his tongue. The boy looked from his father to his mother, and back. They were glaring at one another, but neither spoke another word. All his life, communication between his parents had consisted of such broken sentences, swallowed words, meaningful silences.

Jamie looked at the offending poster. Four men were posing for the camera. One of them, with his plucked eyebrows and pouting lips, did indeed look like a woman. Below them were the words: Culture Club 1982. 'Do You Really Want to Hurt Me?'

'Good question,' Jamie muttered as he opened the window and climbed on to the window-ledge. An it's-still-not-too-late-to-turn-back thought flashed through his head as he crouched on the sill, ready to jump. But it was. It was. The Real-to-Reel Picture Show was waiting for him. *It'll change your life!* Rory McCrory had told him.

How could he *not* go?

—2—
INTO THE NIGHTMARE

'Jamie!' Fiona squealed. 'You made it!'

'We saved a seat for you,' said Alex, 'though we weren't sure you'd be coming.'

'I nearly didn't,' Jamie admitted, and went on to explain how he had defied his father and slipped out of the house without his knowing.

'You didn't!' gasped Fiona, staring at him with obvious admiration.

'I did,' Jamie said, warming to the theme. 'I thought, I am *not* going to miss the show, and I opened the window and ran all the way here. I pushed it to,' he added, 'so I can climb back in later. I just hope they don't notice.'

He fell silent as he was struck by the enormity of what he'd done. How would he be punished if his father did find out?

It was too late to worry about that now. The projector was already whirring into action and the lights were being switched off. Jamie glanced at his watch. On the dot of seven. If he was still at home, he would either be filling in

17

yet more trivial details of Dougall Street in his diary, or reading one of the two books Mr MacDonald allowed him in his room. Eager that Jamie should understand both his body and soul, he had bought him a copy of Gray's *Anatomy* and an Authorized Version of the Bible. Occasionally, Jamie would smuggle in a detective novel which he would read under the covers, but the previous night the torchlight had turned orange and died. He wouldn't be able to buy more batteries until his next pocket-money.

The other kids could stay up and watch television. Alex and Fiona were even allowed to watch the ten-thirty horror film on a Thursday night. Still, the Real-to-Reel Picture Show was guaranteed to out-horror even the spine-tingliest of films. Jamie settled back in his chair, determined not to let anything spoil the evening.

9 8 7. Numbers had appeared on the screen, counting down to the start of the film. 6 5 4. The cone of light shone through the darkness, turning the white canvas a dazzling silver. 3. From various points in the hall, children coughed nervously. 2. Silence descended. 1. Jamie shuddered involuntarily and gripped the arm-rests tightly, as the screen was suddenly filled with the sinister opening scene.

There was a forest: a dank and dismal pine-forest, where next to no light penetrated the overhead canopy of bottle-green. Nothing stirred. No bird sang. The thick mattress of khaki pine-needles on the ground muffled the unmistakable sound of something approaching.

The children in the audience looked on in horror. Jamie heard Fiona give a little shriek as the ominous rustling grew louder, as whatever it was got nearer. The sound of a sharp intake of breath and a pounding heart filled the hall as the lost child in the forest realized that someone was in pursuit.

You never saw the face of the victim. The camera recorded everything through his or her eyes, darting from this to that, hovering for an instant on something else, before once more trying to penetrate the gloomy shadows to discover what was lurking there. It heightened the terrifying suspense: every boy and girl knew exactly what it would be like if *they* were trapped in the evil wood.

Without any warning, a new sound started up: it was the high-pitched screech of a chain-saw. The unseen character in the film began running blindly through the trees, the camera capturing every terrified twist and turn, every panicked footstep as the child ran ever deeper into the dense forest. Thicker and thicker became the undergrowth. Jagged thorns, as sharp as talons, lashed out wildly, tearing at soft skin.

The hall was filled with a cacophony of noise as the chain-saw whined, the victim wailed and a sudden wind whisked across the pine-needles on the forest floor.

Suddenly, the camera stopped, jerked round, surveyed the scene for any possible way out. There was none. It went to move again — but could not. The brambles had seized the opportunity to wrap themselves tightly round the child's legs, and the howling wind had already caused the pine-needles to drift up over the knees.

'Can't move,' a breathless voice announced. 'Can't get free.'

Again the camera looked round. It came to rest on the severed branch of a nearby tree. The wood was white, and fresh sawdust was sprinkled over the ground. The camera panned in on a droplet of resin trickling over the bark. Closer and closer it went; close enough to see that it wasn't resin at all. It was blood.

Someone in the hall screamed. Fiona bit deeply into her lower lip. Alex leant forward, transfixed by the sight of the deep-red, glutinous blood, pumping down the branch and pouring over the trunk.

'No!' the voice screamed.

The camera swung round and focused on a movement in

the shadows. The dazzling glint of razor-sharp steel heralded the arrival of the attacker. He was masked; he was sitting in a motorized wheelchair; he was wielding a massive chain-saw, waving it round his head like a warrior a sword. The camera looked deep into the man's cold, pitiless eyes. There could be no thought of mercy.

'A wheelchair,' the voice whispered. 'I could escape, I could run faster than . . . if only I could release my legs. If only I could break free,' and the sounds of frantic scrabbling at the pine-needles and wrenching at the savage brambles echoed round the hall.

Jamie gnawed at his thumb nail. He couldn't watch. He couldn't turn away.

All the children were petrified. All of them identified with the plight of the child trapped in the forest, being attacked by a madman. And as the wheelchair lurched forwards, and the screeching chain-saw sliced through the air, every single boy and girl screamed in mortal terror.

But there was one particular child in the audience for whom the scene was more than an episode from a horror film. There was one child who had recognized the setting from the very beginning, who had watched in fascinated dread as the sequence of events had unfolded. He remembered the dark forest; he had known the chain-saw would start up when it did; he felt the familiar shudder of disgust as the severed branch began to bleed. He recognized the minutest detail of each and every frame of the film – for this was his dream.

Haunted by the recurring nightmare for years, Liam Donahue – the boy Jamie had watched passing his house half an hour earlier – now found himself at its very centre. For this is the way that *Rory McCrory's Real-to-Reel Picture Show* worked.

Unlike an ordinary cinema, where the projectionist loads up the latest New York thriller or Hollywood comedy, the reels that Rory McCrory clipped into place were blank. He was there to record film, not to show it. The scenes the children were watching had never been seen by a public audience before. They were the private fears, the inner hurt, the emotions too fragile to be revealed; all twisted into hideous dreams that returned just often enough to make sleep itself a nightmare.

For Liam Donahue, the sight of his own dream splashed across the screen was the greatest release he had ever known. He never remembered the nightmare when he woke up. He had never been allowed to think about it logically. Suddenly he could see it for what it was — a cheap scene from a video nasty.

And yet, despite being awake, the terror was no less intense. At the sight of the madman, he had pulled his feet up on to the seat and hugged his knees tightly to his chest. As the chain-saw rose above the man's head, the dream suddenly lost its familiarity. This was the point where he would wake up, dripping in sweat, writhing frantically to avoid the descending blade.

Liam began to panic. What was going to happen now? How would the nightmare finally end?

Rory McCrory was proud of his Real-to-Reel Picture Show. He had invented the machine, which was able to project dreams on to the screen, some thirty-five years ago. He'd called it a Traumascope, and since then he'd been on the road, travelling from place to place, giving unhappy children the opportunity to confront their worst nightmares. But, as Rory McCrory would always stress, he was not merely a 'brilliant' inventor — modesty was never one of his strong points — but also a psychologist, a therapist, a healer. When he realized what he had created, McCrory saw in the contraption the potential not merely to entertain, but also to cure troubled young minds.

'This one ought to do,' he said, selecting a suitable ending for the hideous fantasy on the screen, and slotting the strip of film into place.

'Perfect,' he whispered, as the reel flawlessly took over from the gruesome climax of Liam Donahue's nightmare.

The children in the hall held their breath as the camera focused on the descending blade. The screeching whine intensified, battling it out with the howling wind.

All at once, the sky was alive with jagged fingers of blue lightning scraping across the sky and hurtling down to the forest floor. One stray fire-bolt pierced through the branches and speared down into the base of the tallest pine tree. There was a loud hiss and a cloud of smoke and steam. Then a crack, followed immediately by a long, protracted creak: the sound of a heavy oak door swinging open on unoiled hinges.

None of the boys or girls in the audience dared even blink as the pine began to sway – first this way, then that. The madman too appeared mesmerized by the tree. In his increasingly desperate attempts to anticipate precisely where the tree would fall, he propelled his wheelchair forwards, slammed it into reverse; he shifted from the left to the right, and back again.

And then the waiting was over. The tree wavered no longer. It was coming down, slicing through the air with impossible speed, snapping off the branches of its neighbours like matchsticks. The madman in the wheelchair never stood a chance. In less than the time it takes to clap your hands, the massive pine had crashed down upon the evil attacker.

The camera captured the instant of disbelief in the madman's eyes as the tree struck. And then he was gone. As the ferocious storm abated and the wind died away, the camera looked down. There was the tree, embedded in the thick carpet of pine-needles – but that was all. No trace of anything else: no madman, no wheelchair, no chain-saw. They had all disappeared.

For ever.

Pandemonium reigned in the hall as the boys and girls cheered, clapped, whooped, whistled and yelled their approval of the final scene. Everything had turned out fine in the end. As it always did. As it always would.

In the middle of the third row, however, was one boy who was not cheering, who was not clapping. He was shaking with relieved laughter. Having seen the end of the nightmare at last, he knew there was nothing more to fear. Never again could its morbid horror infiltrate his dreams.

His nightmare was over: consigned to the past. From then on, Liam Donahue would sleep peacefully at night.

But there were still many more nightmares to cure. The Traumascope was once again at work, probing into the subconscious minds of the children and picking out the most distressed images from the depths of their buried memories. Already, the picture on the screen was quite different. The dark, forbidding forest had disappeared and in its place was a golden autumn afternoon. There was a swollen river, tumbling over jagged rocks which had been stepping-stones before the heavy rains. A crooked weeping willow, its roots clutching on to the muddy bank, grew out over the swirling water.

It is the atmosphere of a nightmare which remains. Even though none of the details can be recalled on waking, the *feel* of the dream persists. 'It was purple-red and silken.' 'There was an awful heaviness; sombre, immovable.' 'Dirty and disgusting like ... like the stained scum fanning out from a factory waste-pipe.' Trying to put into words the uniqueness of that atmosphere is impossible: it cowers deep inside the child, who has emerged trembling from the nightmare, and will not be described.

But it was the atmosphere of that quiet river scene which Jamie had instantly recognized. It was chilly, despite the sun. It was a shade of acid yellow, harsh and sour, as if he were watching the entire scene through a tinted window. Like glass, the dream was ominously brittle; the tranquillity of the river bank threatening to shatter and form a million vicious splinters. Jamie remained transfixed. Even when the feeling of dread increased, he was unable to avert his gaze from the screen, unable to impede the inevitable progress of his nightmare.

'No,' he murmured weakly, as the camera looked down and showed two podgy feet stirring up the mud in the shallows. 'I can't,' he gasped. 'Not this. I can't!'

Intent on the film, Fiona and Alex were unaware of Jamie's agitation. They didn't realize how clammy his skin had become, or how dry his mouth. They didn't know how their friend's pounding heart beat faster and faster as the camera moved up the length of the weeping willow.

It paused for a moment on a message newly carved into the bark. There was a heart, pierced with an arrow. At the top were the letters M.M.; at the bottom F.J. The camera continued its ascent. A girl's shoes were revealed; bare legs, striped shorts, a faded lilac vest bearing the photograph of a pop group, soft, brown hair resting on bony shoulders, and then the face.

Those beautiful blue eyes staring back at Jamie. Instinctively, he shut his own eyes to blank out their imploring gaze. But the juddering panic continued. His entire body was trembling, quaking: he knew that his very survival was in danger. He was being shaken apart by the onslaught of memory.

At the back of the hall, from his position behind the projector, Rory McCrory had noticed what was taking place at once. The light from the Traumascope was pouring down into the boy, enclosing him in its pocket of dazzling energy and tugging him towards the screen.

'Not this again,' McCrory whispered. For he had witnessed the same phenomenon once before.

He had once taken the Real-to-Reel Picture Show to the Isle of Arran. There, a red-haired girl called Elizabeth McNulty had been watching the films, when her turn had come to relive her worst nightmare. But something had gone wrong. Unlike the other children, whose memories surrendered the dream only too willingly, Elizabeth refused to let go. The Traumascope was equally stubborn, however, and far stronger. Programmed to reveal the nightmare in its entirety, whatever might occur, its beam had held the girl as firmly as a dentist's pliers grips a decayed tooth. She had withstood the force as long as she could, but the battle was one-sided. Losing concentration for an instant, she had found herself on the other side of the screen.

Elizabeth McNulty had never been seen again.

That had been twenty years ago. Now, on the island of Skye, it was happening all over again. Rory McCrory looked on helplessly as his invention carried on, out of control. He tried unplugging the machine — as he had the time before — but it had no effect. The energy already generated was sufficient for the Traumascope to complete its task.

Jamie opened his eyes to find himself encased in light. He yelled at his friends for help — but no sound penetrated the thick brightness. Why didn't they notice him? Why couldn't they see what was happening? He tried to reach out to them, but the light restrained him. Above his head, the main beam continued to shine down on the screen, where the girl in the tree was saying something into the camera and laughing. But the cables of light between the beam and the trapped boy were becoming stronger. And as his body continued to tremble, Jamie felt himself being drawn upwards, atom by atom by atom.

Suddenly he realized he was no longer sitting in his seat. He was standing on the beam itself, staring down towards the screen.

'NOOOO!' he screamed, but his last desperate plea remained unheard, as he hurtled down the dazzling slope and into his nightmare.

The Traumascope stopped and the hall was plunged into darkness. Several children shrieked, thinking this must be a part of the film. But when the houselights came back on, they realized something was wrong and turned to one another in surprise and disbelief.

Surely that couldn't be all. Only one and a quarter scenes: that wasn't *nearly* enough. What was going on?

'I'm afraid that due to a technical problem beyond my control, this evening's performance has ended,' Rory Mc-Crory was saying.

Shocked silence greeted his announcement. A moment later the hall was filled with angry boos and cat-calls. A chant of 'we want more, we want more,' was soon echoing round the hall. But McCrory was not in the mood for a rebellion.

'DESIST!' he roared.

The noise instantly ceased.

> *Alas, my friends, the time has come to go,*
> *Too much of a bad thing isn't good, you know,*
> *But if the Real-to-Reel has helped you grow,*
> *Come back next year for a brand-new Picture Show.*

Rory McCrory would be the first to admit that his rendition of the farewell verse hadn't been sincerely delivered. He had spat the words out, with his eyes glaring threateningly. All he wanted to do was get the kids out of the hall and be on his own.

He needed to think. He needed to decide whether or not

he should ever use the Traumascope again. Yes, certainly he had helped countless hundreds of boys and girls over the years, but at what cost? Two children had now disappeared. What happened if, like Elizabeth McNulty, this boy proved unable to escape from the nightmare?

The fact was that Rory McCrory's invention was more powerful than its inventor. It had a mind – or a purpose – of its own, and nothing he could do was enough to prevent it taking control. McCrory stared miserably at the empty chair, willing the boy to reappear.

'Please come back, please, please!' But he knew it was hopeless. The boy had disappeared and he, the so-called healer, was responsible.

When it became clear that Rory McCrory was not about to change his mind about the evening's performance, the hall began to empty.

'I'm going to ask for my money back,' said Fiona indignantly.

'Oh, leave it,' said Alex. 'If the machine *is* broken, there's nothing he can do about it and . . .'

'I don't believe it is,' Fiona interrupted.

'And even if it isn't,' Alex continued, 'there's no way we can prove it.'

'Well, I still don't think it's . . . Where's Jamie?'

Alex turned and looked at the empty seat.

'Did you see him leaving?'

'No, he was right here a minute ago.'

'Where is he then?'

Fiona jumped up on the seat and looked round the hall, scrutinizing each of the boys as they made their way towards the exit. Jamie was not among them.

'See him?' Alex asked.

'No, I . . .'

Just then Fiona noticed Rory McCrory. At first, she

thought he was looking at her and she glowered back, to show how displeased she was with the outcome of the cinema show. McCrory didn't respond and Fiona realized with a jolt that he wasn't looking at her at all. He was staring at the chair next to hers: the empty chair, the chair where Jamie had been sitting. Her heart began to pound furiously.

At that moment their eyes did meet, and Fiona noted the look of panic which passed across Rory McCrory's face. It wasn't like him. Usually he was so jolly and sure of himself. Suddenly, he looked like a naughty little boy, who had been caught doing something he knew he shouldn't. McCrory's fear and guilt were unmistakable. For that instant, *she* knew that *he* knew that *she* knew that *he* knew something about Jamie's disappearance.

Fiona felt uncharacteristically frightened. She dropped back down to the floor.

'He knows something,' she hissed.

'Who?'

'McCrory. He's done something with Jamie. I know he has.'

'Fiona McKintosh,' said Alex. 'Your imagination's so fertile, you could grow roses in it!' It was something their mum was always saying. Normally it would make Fiona smile. But not now. She couldn't forget that expression of guilty terror. Fiona was convinced that Rory McCrory knew where Jamie was.

'Don't you remember the message?' she said. *'It'll change your life!* It was meant for Jamie, not us!'

'But how?' Alex asked quietly. He didn't like the situation at all. It was too big to take in, as if the horrors of adult life had suddenly imposed themselves on the sanctuary of the hall, where no one over the age of fourteen was allowed.

'What do we do now?' he said. His voice was trembling.

'I don't know,' Fiona admitted. 'We'll just have to hope Jamie's safe — wherever he is.'

—3—

IN PURSUIT

When Fiona and Alex finally decided to follow Rory Mc-Crory, it was because they couldn't think of a better course of action.

'We can't go and tell his parents,' Fiona said. 'Old Mac-Donald'd kill us. You know what he's like.'

Alex nodded glumly. 'And I'm not going to the police.'

'No,' Fiona agreed. 'Not until we've got some proof anyway. They'd probably just laugh at us.'

The situation they were in was becoming more night-marish than any of the scenes from the picture show. They stood shivering outside the hall, waiting for McCrory to appear. All the other kids had gone home and the street was deserted. As if to spite them, the weather had turned nasty again and a fine, stinging drizzle was lashing their faces with each icy gust.

'What do you think he's doing?'

'Packing up.'

'Well, what's taking him so long?' Fiona asked irritably.

'I'm freezing.'

'Sssh!' Alex hissed and pulled himself back out of sight behind the telephone-box.

The side-door swung open and Rory McCrory emerged, Traumascope in one hand, box of reels in the other. Under his left arm was the rolled-up screen. He turned left and went round the back of the building to the car-park.

Alex and Fiona watched him, memorizing his every physical characteristic, in case the police should need a detailed description. He was of below-average height, but extremely stocky. His hair was black and wavy, his beard a shade lighter. Eyes, piercing blue and deep-set; nose thin; lips narrow. A thick gold ring hung from his left ear. There was something odd about the way he walked. While not limping exactly, his right foot would move slightly awkwardly, as if a broken ankle had been set badly. He was wearing a thick jumper, jeans, boots, a donkey jacket, with a red spotted kerchief tied around his neck.

Darting from phone-box to tree, crouching behind a garden wall, racing down the Tarmac path in the shadow of the hall, Fiona and Alex followed McCrory, anxious not to let him get away. They had convinced themselves that if they once let him out of their sight, they would never see their friend Jamie again — at least, not alive.

'Evening, Major,' McCrory greeted his horse. 'Certainly brought the house down this evening, didn't we?' he added, and sighed deeply. 'Keep your hoofs crossed, it'll all turn out all right!'

'Did you hear that?' Fiona whispered. 'I told you he knew something.'

'It would hardly stand up in court,' Alex replied. '"We heard him telling his horse, your Honour."'

'Oh, be quiet,' Fiona said sharply.

She looked at the beautiful old-fashioned gypsy caravan,

with its yellow steps and carved, red balustrade; its slatted shutters and black, cowled chimney. The sturdy grey horse, tethered to the side of the caravan, completed the illusion that Fiona and Alex were staring into the past. Only the gentle thrum of the generator, which provided electricity for McCrory's heating and lighting, confirmed that they hadn't somehow been transported back to a time before the invention of the internal combustion engine.

McCrory climbed the wooden steps which led up to the door. He struggled for a moment — trying to balance the Traumascope, the case of reels and the screen, while getting the key in the lock — before disappearing inside and out of sight.

Without saying a word, Alex and Fiona made for the caravan windows, creeping over the gravel as quietly as they could. The horse tried its best to give them away, but the nosebag muffled its fretful neighing.

Nearly there, Alex thought, his heart thumping.

When they did arrive, the windows were too high to look through. Luckily, however, McCrory had parked the caravan next to the chain fence, and there were two conveniently placed posts for the children to climb on to. Balancing precariously on one foot, Alex pulled himself up. He caught a tantalizing glimpse of a luxurious interior, decorated with crimson velvet, mahogany and gold, before the curtains were drawn abruptly in front of his eyes. Not even the slightest crack remained for him to peer through. A moment later, the same thing occurred to Fiona at the next window.

'And now?' Alex asked as he jumped down.

'Let's give it a while longer,' Fiona said. 'Just see what happens.'

They didn't have long to wait, which was just as well, as the vicious weather was making their vigil almost intolerable. Scarcely ten minutes after slamming the door shut, McCrory re-emerged. He removed the horse's nosebag and clanked down a bucket of water. The animal whinnied appreciatively.

'See you later, Major, me old matie,' McCrory said.

> *'I'm off to town for a pint of beer,*
> *I'll see you again at the start of next year.'*

'Quick,' said Alex, 'what do we do?'

'I'll follow him,' Fiona said, instantly taking control of the situation. 'You get into the caravan while I'm away. See if you can find any clues.'

'What sort of clues?'

'Oh, Alex!' she said — for an older brother, he could certainly be a bit wet at times. 'I've got to go, otherwise I'll lose him. Just see if there's anything that might help us find Jamie.'

She sped after McCrory as he disappeared round the corner.

'She's so bossy,' Alex muttered as he stomped off, looking for a way in to the caravan. The front door was out of the question; McCrory had double-locked it before leaving. And the windows were all bolted.

'This is hopeless,' Alex said. Determined to prove he wasn't as useless as his sister maintained, however, he continued his search.

There was a second door at the back of the caravan. Made of the same red and yellow panelling as the rest of the wagon, it blended in perfectly with the sides. Only the knob gave it away. Alex tugged at it. The last thing he had expected was that the door would be unlocked, and when it jerked open, Alex let out a little cry of surprise. The horse whinnied again.

Checking first that he wasn't being watched, the boy slipped inside the dark caravan. He found himself in a small but well-stocked kitchen. Copper pans hung from hooks, a set of knives glinted from magnets above the cooker, earthenware pots bristled with whisks, ladles and wooden spoons. Glass jars containing spaghetti, macaroni, brown and white rice, lentils and beans, lined the shelves; above them were racks of corked bottles labelled sage, thyme, oregano, cumin and dill. A huge leg of ham hung from a butcher's hook.

Alex shuddered and made his way through into the main area of the caravan. The impression of sumptuous comfort that he had glimpsed through the window was confirmed. The room was ornately decorated with maroon satin and tasselled velvet. Intricately carved statuettes stared down at him from the corners; gold edging and brass lamps shone in the dim light.

'Wow!' Alex muttered.

His attention was drawn to a shelf running the length of the left-hand wall. A display of weird instruments, apparatuses and mechanical devices was arranged along it. Alex approached nervously. The things looked harmless enough, but you could never be too careful.

The first object consisted of a brass handle shaped like the letter Y: a brass disc was attached by a pin to the two forks. Alex picked it up and looked more closely. On one side of the disc was a crouching man; on the other was a second man in mid-air, his arms and legs outstretched. Alex flicked the disc and the man began to jump – up, down, up, down.

Clever, thought Alex, laying it aside.

The next contraption was too big to pick up. There was a white cylinder with numerous figures of a clown painted round the inside. They were in the various stages of juggling. By turning a handle on the left, the drum began to rotate.

'That's not much cop,' Alex said, as the little men blurred together. But then, noticing a slit in the outer casing of the machine, he bent down and peeked through. The magic was made visible. As the drum spun, the little figures became a single performer, juggling his skittles, dropping one, bending to retrieve it and starting all over.

Alex smiled, staring intently at the apparent movement in the pictures of the clown he knew were perfectly motionless. It was mesmeric, the black and white flashing through the narrow slit, and Alex pulled away nervously.

'Don't want to hypnotize yourself,' he said. 'Perhaps that's what he does — bewitches children with these apparent toys, and then, when they are in his power, he kidnaps and enslaves them.' Even Alex realized that he was letting his imagination run a bit too far away with him.

'You're getting as bad as Fiona,' he told himself.

He moved on to the next item: an old-fashioned camera with a leather concertina extension at the front. A black cloth hung down limply at the back.

'Cheese!' Alex said, and grinned into the lens.

Fiona had soon guessed where McCrory was heading.

'Well might you have a drink,' she muttered as he disappeared into the Royal Hotel.

Standing on the pavement opposite, Fiona watched the shadowy silhouette through the frosted glass as McCrory approached the bar and stopped. A blurred arm was raised, the head jerked backwards, and the arm was lowered. A moment later the action was repeated. And again. McCrory was clearly not drinking beer.

Fiona made a mental note: Suspect agitated.

It occurred to her that there was little point staying any longer. Jamie wasn't here. McCrory had merely come into town for a drink — or three. She ought to get back and help Alex search the caravan properly; he was bound to miss the vital piece of evidence.

At that moment, McCrory appeared at the door of the

hotel. Pausing for a moment to pull his collar up against the wind, he set off back to the caravan. Fiona gasped. If McCrory caught her brother in his caravan, who knew what he might do? She had to get back. She had to warn him. Otherwise Jamie wouldn't be the only boy to go missing that night.

McCrory was already on the main road. Fiona's heart pounded furiously. She couldn't simply run past him. Her only hope was to go the back way. If she was lucky, the fierce head-wind and McCrory's injured foot would delay him just long enough for her to reach Alex in time.

She raced up a narrow side alley and round past the post office. Hardly noticing the worsening weather, she sped over the cracked and uneven paving-stones with the sure-footedness of a mountain goat. Leaping a puddle, she veered to the left and careered across the square to the hall. Surely McCrory couldn't have made it yet, even though his route was shorter.

'Alex, Alex, Alex,' she called as loudly as she dared.

But there was no response from the caravan.

'ALEX!'

She jumped up at one of the windows and slapped it with her hand. The horse whinnied loudly.

'ALEX!'

The curtain moved and she saw her brother waving down at her.

'Get out, quick,' she said, in a husky stage whisper.

Alex cupped his hand to his ear, equally theatrically, and feigned a look of extreme puzzlement. Then, as if suddenly understanding, he pointed behind him — the back door is open, he mouthed silently.

'The boy's a halfwit,' Fiona muttered as she raced round to the back of the caravan.

'Alex, get out!' she yelled in through the door. 'Quick!'

'Just come and look at this,' he said.

'There isn't time!' Fiona insisted. 'He's coming.'

The caravan jolted as Major, panicked by the sudden commotion, reared up as far as the tethered reins would allow. He neighed furiously and pounded his hoofs into the gravel.

'ALEX!!'

'OK, OK, I'm . . .'

Alex's reluctant decision to comply with his sister's demands was drowned out by the voice of Rory McCrory himself. He was back.

'Whoa, Major. Whoa, lad,' he called from the far side of the car-park. 'Seen a rat, have you? A nasty human rat prying into my affairs?'

Fiona felt her blood chill. There was still time for her to run and save herself, but she couldn't go home without Alex: what would she tell her parents? And yet, if she went into the caravan now, both of them would be trapped. Then again, they might still make it — McCrory would need at least thirty seconds to unlock the door.

All these thoughts whizzed round her head in an instant. She dived in through the door, and on into the central room. Alex was standing next to a silver and black stroboscope. It was whirring and a bright flashing light filled the entire room. Even in the curious light, Fiona could see that Alex was petrified. The colour had drained from his face. He couldn't move.

Fiona leapt towards the machine — at least, leap is what she tried. Grasped by the strobe, she felt her body lose momentum. Every movement became exaggeratedly slow as if she were walking on the moon; as if she were wading through treacle.

'Got to switch it off,' she mumbled through resolutely clenched teeth.

Her arm stretched down, impossibly slowly, and grasped

at the plug. She pulled it out of its socket and the machine ground to a halt.

Alex gasped. 'I couldn't . . . I . . .'

'Never mind about that,' Fiona said. 'Come on.'

But they were out of luck. It hadn't taken McCrory thirty seconds to get in. It hadn't taken him any time at all. He had come in the back door instead.

'Who's there?' he shouted from the kitchen.

'Quick,' Fiona whispered urgently and grabbed her brother's sleeve.

They disappeared behind the thick curtain at one end of the caravan as McCrory appeared at the other. Finding themselves in a smaller room, they looked round. The bad news was that there was no way out; the good news was that there was a leather and wicker chest large enough to hide the pair of them. Without saying a word, they jumped inside and let the lid close on top of them.

'Gotcha!' McCrory roared as he pulled back the curtain. There was a moment of confused silence. 'Hmm, coulda sworn . . .' he said, looking round the obviously empty room.

'A dram too many of the hard stuff,' he muttered and turned to leave.

Fiona and Alex heard him clump through the neighbouring room. He paused for a moment, apparently inspecting something. Alex pushed the lid open slightly. The sound of McCrory's footsteps on the kitchen floor drifted back. The back door slammed. Then, to their horror, the two children heard the unmistakable metallic click of a key turning in a lock. Rory McCrory had barred their only means of escape.

They looked at each other. Did McCrory know they were there? Even the shadowy darkness could not disguise their dismay. And when the caravan lurched into motion, Alex gave a little scream.

'Where do you think we're going?' he asked.

Fiona merely shrugged. Fearing the worst, however, she chewed her fingernails nervously as the caravan jolted its way downhill. And as the sound of the waves crashing down on the harbour wall grew louder, Fiona knew her suspicions had been correct. McCrory was planning to leave the island as soon as possible.

'Evening, Dougie,' the children heard as the caravan came to a standstill.

'Evening, Rory. Dreadful weather we're having.'

'Seen worse,' said McCrory. 'Still, the journey'll probably take longer than usual, so we'd better get loaded up pretty smartish.'

'Not sure I'm that happy about taking the boat out,' Dougie said slowly. 'Sea's that choppy.'

'We *are* leaving,' said McCrory matter-of-factly. 'There's no question about that. I've got to be on Uist by the morning.'

'But —'

'No buts,' said McCrory. 'It's my boat and my decision. We're going. I can always get a new skipper for the *Ben-Davy*,' he added, and chuckled humourlessly.

Fiona and Alex were in a dilemma. If Rory McCrory *did* know they were there, then he was deliberately abducting them. And if that was the case, then the children ought to use the opportunity to shout to the boatman that they were trapped inside the caravan. On the other hand, if he *didn't* know they were there, the possibility still remained that they might find out what had happened to Jamie. Fiona decided they should keep quiet. After all, Dougie was probably in league with McCrory anyway.

The horse was led over the wobbly gangplank and the solid ground immediately gave way to the pitching swell of the sea. Even in the sheltered harbour, the boat was being tossed around like a cork.

Fiona and Alex heard the engine splutter into action and the wet ropes landing on the deck. They were off. Despite their predicament, Fiona couldn't suppress the rush of excitement she always felt when setting out from the island on a trip.

'Come on,' said Fiona, irritatingly cheerful, 'let's see what's going on outside.'

Easier said than done: having left the relative calm of the bay, the boat had been struck by the full blast of the storm. It rose up on the peaks of the waves, hovered there for an instant, before dropping down into the troughs so fast that Alex and Fiona's stomachs turned. It was like going down in a lift. With the little vessel pitching backwards and forwards, and from side to side, walking the dozen or so feet from the chest to the window became a major expedition. Clutching at anything screwed down, the two children inched their way across the floor. The curious contraptions on the shelf slid this way and that; the pots and pans clattered and banged in the kitchen; foamy waves crashed against the windows. Once, Fiona lost her footing, staggered drunkenly for a couple of seconds, before hurtling across the room and landing in a heap on the sofa.

'You OK?' Alex said.

'Perfect,' Fiona grinned and pulled herself up on to her feet. 'Nice soft landing.'

Alex turned his back and made a dash for the window. He'd gone along with Fiona's decision not to call for help, but he was far from happy. As he looked out, he saw Rory McCrory leaning against the safety rail, swigging from a bottle of wine; beyond him, the sea writhed and frothed like a rabid dog. Fiona had finally made it to the window. Alex turned to her.

'Between the devil and the deep blue sea,' he said.

Fiona smiled. It was an expression their dad was always using.

They looked back outside. McCrory had drained the bottle and a trickle of the red wine ran from the corner of his mouth and into his beard. It looked like blood. It wasn't hard to imagine that nestling in the thick, wavy hair beneath his woolly hat were two little horns.

'Literally!' said Fiona quietly. Even she was beginning to have serious doubts about what they had taken on.

As they continued to watch, McCrory removed a pen and a piece of card from inside his jacket. Then, sheltering from the sea-spray as best he could, he proceeded to scrawl a message.

'"*Do come. It'll change your life!*"' Alex said.

Having rolled the invitation into a tight tube, McCrory pushed it down the neck of the empty wine bottle and rammed the cork in as far as it would go. Then, he drew his arm back behind his head and hurled the bottle out into the turbulent water.

'For the next victim,' Fiona whispered, as the fateful message disappeared into the darkness.

—4—

THE LAND OF PERPETUAL DREAMS

If Alex and Fiona thought their situation was bad, at least they knew where they were. True, it was little comfort to remember that you were being tossed around on the open sea somewhere between Skye and Uist, but that was infinitely preferable to what Jamie had to confront.

Bewildered, the boy looked round. One minute he'd been sitting in a hall watching a film; the next, he was standing in the middle of an unknown road. Although it was just gone noon and the sky was cloudless, the towering terraces on both sides had already plunged the street into chilly semi-darkness. Jamie shuddered. There was a staleness in the air, like the cold, dank odour of an unused cellar. It was as if the entire area was rotting; road, houses and all.

There were no turn-offs or alley-ways to break the featureless repetition of wall, windows and doors disappearing into the distance in both directions. There were no people he could ask the way. Jamie stood where he was, not knowing what to do next.

'Hello?' he called. 'Is there anybody there?'

His voice echoed along the street: it sounded as if he had just shouted down a deep, dark tunnel. The question repeated and repeated, but no answer was forthcoming. Jamie hung his head in despair.

'I want to go home,' he muttered miserably. Even the oppressive atmosphere of the MacDonalds' bungalow was preferable to this suburban desolation. But where *was* his home? And how could he get there if he didn't know where he was starting from?

Jamie decided that this problem — immense though it might be — was no reason for doing nothing. And he was just about to begin searching, when the metallic clunk of a door being unbolted caused him to look round. It was impossible to say whether there was any connection between his longing to return home and the sudden activity in the house, but when the big blue door directly in front of him creaked open, Jamie immediately felt more optimistic. The inviting sounds of a noisy party spilled out on to the street.

'At last,' Jamie said and, without even thinking of the consequences of his action, he went inside. Something quite different from common sense was at play here — it was the logic of dreams. There was a door. Doors were for going through. Jamie went through. It was as simple as that.

'Good evening, so glad you could make it,' came a voice.

Jamie turned. A butler dressed in a tail-coat, top hat and bow-tie was standing in front of him, arm outstretched. Jamie shook hands, trying hard not to register surprise at the man's height. He barely came up to Jamie's chest.

'But you haven't got a drink,' he said. 'What can I offer you? Creosote cordial? Emulsion squash? Lacquer liqueur?'

What was the man saying? All the cans and bottles of forbidden, poisonous substances that Mr MacDonald kept under lock and key in the garden shed seemed to be drinks here. Jamie wasn't stupid.

'Have you got any orange juice?' he asked.

'I have,' the man said, looking puzzled, 'but it won't do much to keep the damp out. You'll be rotting away before you can say Jack Robinson. How about a nice white-paint-and-wood-preserver cocktail? It's absolutely delicious.'

'I think I'd still rather prefer orange,' said Jamie.

'So be it,' the man said and hurried off down the corridor. He disappeared into the room where the party was, and slammed the door behind him. The sound of chit-chat and cha-cha music instantly ceased. It was silent. Almost. Jamie became aware of a muffled squeaking coming from the rooms above him.

He waited five minutes. Ten minutes. Evidently the little man was having difficulty locating so exotic a drink for his guest. The high-pitched, grinding squeak grew louder. Another five minutes passed, and the noise became still more insistent. It was like polystyrene on glass, like chalk on a blackboard, like brakes which needed oiling – it was like none of these. Jamie knew he had to investigate and, without waiting for the man to return, he set off up the huge marble staircase.

The walls were lined with gold-framed portraits of men and women with dark, angry eyes. A huge green and pink Chinese vase stood on the first landing. Jamie looked round. The wallpaper was decorated with bamboo; the carpet was a deep, jade green and patterned with cherry blossom. The peculiar squeaking continued: Jamie went up the next flight of stairs.

And the next.

And the next.

With each successive flight, the decoration became simpler, shabbier; the staleness in the air grew more pungent.

By the seventh floor, the threadbare carpets had given way to cracked brown lino, the paper was peeling from the walls and the paintwork was yellowed and chipped. In places, the plaster was falling from the walls and Jamie found he could poke his finger right through. He peered into room after empty room of bare boards, rubble and dust.

'This is horrible,' he whispered, and jumped back as his own words hissed round the landing.

The squeak squealed irritably above him. Why was the boy dilly-dallying? it seemed to demand.

Jamie had thought he was already at the top of the building, but as he turned, he noticed yet another staircase at the far end of the corridor. As he approached it, he knew that he didn't want to go any further; that he shouldn't take another step. The stairs were rickety, the banisters askew, and the wood of which both had been made was in the last stages of decay.

Yet Jamie could not now turn back. He placed one tentative foot on the first step. The wood creaked ominously.

Perhaps that was what I heard, he thought.

But a sharp noise from above his head instantly informed him that it was a squeak and not a creak that he was following. He held on to the banisters grimly, praying that the entire flight would not collapse like a house of cards. At the next landing, there wasn't even lino on the floor. Warped floorboards, riddled with worm, extended down the shadowy hallway.

The state of collapse at the landing after that had reached such a degree that, in places, Jamie could see through to the floor below. He edged his way along the wall to the next flight.

'How much further?' he asked himself, knowing that it was madness to go on; knowing that he was too frightened to go back down the crumbling stairway. He stumbled onwards. The following flight was circular, as was the next; and with each successive ascent, the walls came in closer and closer, until Jamie found himself going round and round in a steep, dark tower. No one had come this way for years, decades, perhaps centuries, and thick, dusty cobwebs wrapped themselves around his face. The sticky filaments wound their way into his ears and eyes, up his nose. He sneezed twice.

'Bless you,' he muttered to himself automatically.

Squeezing through a small, square hole, Jamie emerged on a platform up in the loft. A wooden ladder disappeared above him, reaching up to a point where the four sides of the roof converged. The squeaking seemed to be coming from the very top of the ladder. The logic of the dream dictated that Jamie should climb. He did so.

It wasn't bad at first. The rungs were smooth but firm, and he soon got into a rhythm of left hand and foot, right hand and foot, left hand and foot, over and over. The tiles on the inside of the roof seemed to get no closer. Jamie looked up. The apex was as far above his head as when he had started. He looked down.

This was the fatal mistake. The sight of the tiny platform, miles below him, made his head spin and his legs shake. Suddenly, his grip on the flimsy pieces of wood seemed unsure; his hands and feet became hopelessly uncoordinated. A couple of the rungs he had already passed dislodged themselves and tumbled through the air. An eternity later they clattered to the floor below.

'No, no, no,' Jamie began to pant.

He took a deep breath and continued up the ladder. He wouldn't look down again. The top was only a couple of steps away. He could make it: he *could* make it!

The sound of something large and brittle cracking, ripped through the air like a knife through paper. Jamie froze. For a second nothing happened. Then, with the sound of a storm-tide dragging pebbles down the beach, the tiles began to slide down the roof like the scales washed from a mackerel's back. Dazzling sunlight poured in as huge gaps appeared above him. Stripped of cover, the rafters and beams stood out against the yellow sky like the bones of a gargantuan dinosaur, before they too collapsed and tumbled down into the abyss.

Jamie looked down. What he saw made no sense. The house had gone, and with it the party, the little man and all the flights of stairs. Nothing remained of the scene he had entered.

'But . . .' he said, and his words were carried off by a warm, gentle breeze.

Below him was a curious arrangement of roads – hundreds of them – all radiating from a central point, some way to his left. Each one appeared to consist of a single strip of square, black paving-stones set in white concrete. Poking his head through the rungs and peering directly down, Jamie saw that he and the ladder were extending out of one of the dark slabs. From this altitude, it looked no larger than a postage stamp.

'But I'm not dizzy,' Jamie said.

Usually heights gave him vertigo, but here, enclosed by the sky and rocked by the ladder which was swaying gently to and fro, he felt warm and secure. Above him, Jamie finally managed to locate the source of the mysterious squeaking. A tiny flag was fluttering in the breeze and, as it did so, the thin cable scraped against the varnished mast. The boy knew he had never felt so good.

But the moment could not last. As quickly as a window can shatter, as unexpectedly as a telephone breaks the silence, as threateningly as a smile can disappear, so the atmosphere changed. The flag revealed itself as a pirate's Jolly Roger, and as Jamie watched, the grinning skull leered at him menacingly. Jamie was afraid. Cold air chilled his clammy skin and glued his lank fringe to his forehead. He gripped the slippery wooden struts with sweaty hands as the ladder tottered and lurched further and further out of control.

'Please!' Jamie cried out. 'It can't be!'

But there could be no doubt; he was falling. As the ladder sliced through the air, Jamie screeched, clutched hold of the underside of the rungs and clung on with every bit of strength he possessed. It was so much worse falling backwards, unable to see where he was going to end up. Craning his neck round and back, Jamie found himself speeding over the spoke-like roads and down towards the central hub.

He opened his mouth to scream, but no sound emerged. He screwed his eyes shut.

'Got to wake up, got to wake up,' he muttered, knowing that there was something familiar about the whole episode; knowing that if he didn't wake before he reached the bottom, his heart would stop. That was what everybody said.

Jamie kept his eyes tightly clamped and, as the ladder flew down through the degrees to the horizontal, he waited in terror for the inevitable crash-landing. A sudden image of his own bones shattering into a million pieces flashed before him.

The landing came. It was a shock, suddenly coming to a standstill, but Jamie realized that it hadn't hurt him. Before daring to open his eyes, however, he felt carefully along his legs, over his shoulder, round his face. Everything seemed to be intact.

He sat up and looked round. Directly in front of him was a tall signpost, with arrows pointing off in every direction. Below this was a large blue notice covered in gold writing. Jamie went to investigate.

WELCOME TO THE LAND OF PERPETUAL DREAMS, the board announced.

Jamie took a moment to let the words sink in before continuing.

You are here because you need to be here. However, this fact does nothing to minimize the dangers you face. The utmost caution must be exercised at all times. You are here entirely at your own risk and the governing body shall not be liable in cases of death, mutilation or maiming.

'Blimey,' Jamie mumbled. The task ahead — whatever it might be — seemed daunting, to put it mildly.

But do not be of faint heart. Diligent following of the instructions should result in a successful conclusion to your visit.

1. *Your aim: to locate your own nightmare.*
2. *Do not proceed until you are one hundred per cent sure you are heading in the correct direction.*
3. *Correct direction shall be determined as follows:*
   a. *Select key element to nightmare, e.g. falling, flying, forests, frogs or funerals.*
      (If there are two or more elements, decide the more/most significant.)
   b. *Check category of nightmare on signpost: the subjects have been alphabetically ordered for your convenience.*
   c. *Advance to the appropriate roadway indicated by the arrow.*

Take care! Any mistakes made at this stage could prove fatal.

REMEMBER: ANYTHING CAN HAPPEN — AND PROBABLY WILL!

'It all sounds a wee bit over-dramatic!' Jamie muttered. 'Surely it can't do any harm just to have a quick peek inside a nightmare or two. After all, the falling dream ended up all right.'

He walked towards the edge of the podium and looked round at the roadways extending into the distance in all directions. They looked harmless enough. There were no nightmares to be seen here – presumably the roads led you to them. He wouldn't go too far in, he decided, but he just had to see what it was like in someone else's imagination. Jamie jumped down on to one of the narrow plastic strips and took a few cautious steps forward.

'So far, so good,' he said.

But even as he spoke, the atmosphere had changed and Jamie saw, to his horror, that the road, the podium and the signpost had all disappeared. He found himself standing next to a jumbled heap of polystyrene boxes full of rotting fruit and vegetables. Bruised peaches, black bananas, squelchy marrows and tomatoes: the whole lot stank like a compost heap.

Jamie moved away and looked round at his new surroundings. The scene was one of desolation. Ragwort and rosebay willow-herb grew up between the cracked paving-stones. A rat scuttled this way and that among the abandoned heaps of rubbish, spoilt for choice. Tall soot-darkened walls of disused factories were covered in fading graffiti and layers of torn posters. Barred windows of cracked and grimy glass, rusting gateways, broken lamps and drainpipes told their own story of neglect. The entire industrial estate was like a vast *Marie Celeste*. Not a soul remained.

Jamie suddenly felt desperately alone.

He walked across the concrete forecourts, peering in through broken doors at one empty workshop after another. His footsteps echoed eerily. It was wrong that somewhere so large should be so quiet. He tried to fill his head with songs, to keep the dreadful emptiness at bay. But his father had banned pop music in the house and it was half a verse from that morning's hymn which Jamie repeated over and

49

over: 'There is a green hill far away, without a city wall.' In this deserted wasteland, it was difficult to imagine green hills anywhere.

And then he was struck by a thought which lodged itself in his brain. With absolute certainty, Jamie knew that he was the only person left alive in the world. It wasn't the first time he'd felt so alone. On cold, dark, wintry mornings as he made his way down to the newsagent's for his paper round, he had often imagined that everyone else, everywhere, had vanished. He was the sole survivor of a global catastrophe — until the headlights of an oncoming car would indicate that at least one other person had also escaped the general annihilation.

This time, nothing happened to destroy the feeling of utter isolation. No doctors making early-morning calls, no night-watchmen returning home after their shift, no dustmen emptying bins, no joggers keeping fit. No one at all.

'There's one thing,' he muttered, shocked by the sound of his own voice breaking the silence, 'no one never did someone any harm.'

But Jamie remained unconvinced by this display of irrefutable logic. He didn't like being completely on his own, and so, on hearing the distant sound of whimpering, he immediately headed off towards the potential companion. The logic of dreams had once again taken control.

He didn't really give much thought to what might be making the noise. Perhaps it was an old man who had lost his walking-stick and couldn't leave with the rest. Or a child who had been separated from its parents. Jamie was thinking only of the companionship he longed for. It was for this reason that when he went through the gate and into the yard where the whimpering was coming from, Jamie was totally unprepared for the sight of the furious, slavering creature which confronted him. He leapt back instinctively.

With teeth bared and mouth frothing, the Rottweiler hurled itself through the air at the boy. Jamie remained fixed to the spot, watching petrified as the savage, blood-thirsty face lunged at his own. The dog's warm, foul breath slapped him like a piece of rotten meat. Jamie shuddered with revulsion and staggered back a couple of paces: the dog collapsed at his feet and resumed its pathetic whining.

A piece of rope, fifteen metres long, stretched out across the yard. One end had been secured to the factory gates, the other was attached to a lead. It was only the choke-chain that prevented the animal snarling its rage.

'Poor thing,' Jamie murmured gently. The Rottweiler had clearly been forgotten when everyone else had left. It was starving and the ribs protruding from its stocky body gave the impression that it had swallowed an open umbrella in a last desperate attempt to satisfy its hunger.

He looked at the writhing animal miserably. To survive, the dog would have to be untied, but whoever set the animal free would die for their pains.

'If only there was something I could do to help,' Jamie said.

But you already have, the dog's eyes seemed to reply. You've given me an idea.

The Rottweiler looked away, pulled itself up and trotted back towards the factory, as if it had all the time and not a care in the world. Half-way there, it stopped, laid its paw across the rope and calmly began to gnaw through the thick fibres.

Jamie stared in terrified fascination. It was as though the dog had read his mind. The rope was beginning to fray. If he didn't make a run for it now, he would never escape the dog's fearsome jaws.

Never had Jamie run like he was running now. Neither doing cross-country, nor completing laps of the school playing-fields for football training. This was long-distance sprinting. This was the run-or-be-eaten handicap marathon.

'Keep going,' Jamie instructed his feet, his legs, his lungs, his pumping heart. Before the rope snapped, he needed to get as far away from the Rottweiler as possible. If he was lucky, it would be too weak from lack of food to catch him up. Then he would be able to hide; he would be able to make his escape from this run-down industrial sprawl.

Yet even as he was making plans, Jamie could already feel the vibrations of heavy paws pounding across the cracked concrete, and hear the blood-chilling baying of the ravenous animal in pursuit of its prey. Jamie dared not even glance back over his shoulder. It would waste a valuable milli-millisecond.

He raced past defaced walls, darted along dingy alleys, and hurtled headlong over broken paving-stones, where the weeds and creepers were already in the process of obliterating all trace of human presence. His chest was aching with the strain, his legs were turning to jelly, but the warm deadly breath on the back of his heels enabled him to tap reserves of strength he didn't know he had.

To his right he saw the familiar boxes of rotting vegetables. Just a little further; just a few more yards, he urged himself.

But it was hopeless. The dog's snarling jaws were already snapping at his feet. He looked around desperately for a wall he could scale; for railings he could climb and cling to.

'THIS IS NOT MY NIGHTMARE!' he screamed. The words bounced back off the walls – not my nightmare . . . my nightmare . . . nightmare . . . mare . . . mare . . . mare . . .

Instantly, everything changed. Every movement became an effort, and even though he attempted to continue, the polystyrene boxes remained to his right. But it didn't matter any more. Without even having to look, Jamie knew that the danger had passed. He stopped, bent double and panted uncontrollably. Only when his breathing had returned to normal did he turn round. The Rottweiler had disappeared.

'Not my nightmare,' Jamie repeated quietly. He didn't know what had made him shout the words. But it had worked.

As the Rottweiler had vanished, so too had the atmosphere of the place. Seconds before, the air had been yellow, metallic, threatening − like a razor-sharp blade. Now, the menace was absent and as Jamie looked more closely, the pavements and railings seemed to lose their solidity. He saw the walls for what they were: two-dimensional hardboard constructions, roughly painted to give the impression of bricks and broken windows. Jamie was standing in the middle of an elaborate film-set.

'But it was so real,' he said.

He turned and walked from the scene. The nightmare had lost its power over the boy. Below his feet, the cracked pavement had been replaced with the transparent plastic roadway. This time, however, he noticed something else about the road: he was walking over numbers − one to ten − and there were two rows of rectangular holes running along the edges of the plastic.

'Like a reel of film,' Jamie realized excitedly. 'The nightmares are all stored on film.'

He remembered the view from the top of the ladder: the countless 'roads' that he'd seen, radiating out from that central hub. They weren't roads at all; they were strips of film, each one with its own plot and setting. He looked up: the signpost and notice-board were once again directly ahead. And when he finally reached the end of the plastic strip, Jamie climbed up on to the podium.

'Well, I shan't be trying that again,' he promised himself, trying to make light of his terrifying experience.

Jamie had learnt — the hard way — that the instructions he'd read were not exaggerating. The Land of Perpetual Dreams was indeed a dangerous place. Before setting off in search of his own nightmare, he decided to return to the notice-board and read everything through once more. Jamie had been careless, but it would be the last time.

He reread the notice and then, just to be on the safe side, he read it once again.

Not until he was completely satisfied that he had grasped each and every instruction did he finally make his way to the signpost. With the start of his nightmare still fresh in his mind from the Real-to-Reel Picture Show, he knew precisely which category he had to find.

WAR. WARDROBE. WAREHOUSE. WARTS. WASHING. WASPS. WATCHES...

Watches? Jamie paused to check he'd read the word correctly. Yes, watches it was. How could anyone have bad dreams about watches? But Jamie realized that the connotations and associations the word might have for the suffering dreamer could be totally disproportionate to the object itself — in a nightmare, even the most innocent of memories could become infused with malevolence. He continued down the Ws.

'Water,' Jamie said, coming to his own key-word.

The category of dream was sub-divided into a further four sections: River, Sea, Swimming-pools and Lack Of. Remembering the sunny autumn afternoon and the weeping-willow tree over the running water, Jamie made his choice. WATER (River), it was to be.

He aligned himself with the direction of the arrow on the signpost and fixed his eyes on the length of film straight ahead. Taking care not to allow himself even to blink, Jamie advanced towards the reel. The words of caution on the notice came back to him: *Take care! Any mistakes made at this stage could prove fatal.*

Jamie *had* taken care. He knew now how dangerous it could be if he again entered the wrong dream. The last thing he needed was another encounter with a crazed dog — or a blood-sucking vampire, fire-breathing dragon, marauding pack of wolves, or whatever other horrendous nightmares might be lurking in the reels of film. He would just have to keep his fingers crossed that nothing went wrong — not that they would be much use if it did.

'Here goes nothing,' Jamie said as he reached the beginning of the reel. Doubts instantly began to torment him. Was he a hundred per cent positive this was the right category?

There was only one way to find out, Jamie decided. Without even stopping, he stepped down off the circular platform and on to the clear plastic which, he hoped, would reveal the key to the secrets of his own hideous nightmare.

—5—

NOWHERE TO HIDE

Rory McCrory and Dougie Drew, his skipper, had stayed up all night as the little boat had pitched and rolled across the narrow but treacherous stretch of water between the two islands. While Dougie had kept his hand on the wheel, McCrory had busied himself on deck; ensuring the ropes holding the caravan in place were secure, tending to the nervous horse, keeping a constant check that the unrelenting bombardment of waves was not causing any crucial damage. He also found time to drain another of the bottles of claret and, having written out a second personal invitation to his Real-to-Reel Picture Show, he hurled it out to sea.

The storm was mean. Rory McCrory would be the last person on earth to admit to making a mistake, but even he was shocked by the violence of the elements. The rain thrashed, the waves crashed and the wind, howling and whimpering like a hungry dog, pawed at the squeaking ropes in an effort to dislodge the impudent boat's cargo.

'Shan't be sorry to reach land,' McCrory yelled over the continuous roar.

Dougie merely nodded. Not that he was one to say 'I told you so', but well, he had, hadn't he? They'd be lucky to reach their destination unscathed.

Alex and Fiona had also managed to stay awake, though their task had been harder. Whereas the vicious wind and icy spray had prevented McCrory from becoming drowsy, even for a minute, the warm, cosy caravan soon had the two children rubbing their eyes sleepily. It would be so nice to spread out on the sofas and drift off, but they both knew how foolhardy that would be. If possible, they would slip out of the caravan once they reached dry land. McCrory need never know he had been followed.

But as the hours passed, Alex and Fiona had to shake one another increasingly often as, first one and then the other, would start to nod off.

'I'm shattered,' Alex complained.

'Well, that's tough,' said Fiona sharply. 'It's only one night without sleep and if we do find Jamie, we'll be heroes.'

Alex shrugged and stared out into the night. All he could see was the crest of the nearest wave, its foam stained with yellow from the lamps of the *Ben-Davy*. Beyond that, there was nothing. No sea, no sky — no sign that anything at all existed within the darkness. It was little wonder that centuries ago, sailors believed that if you sailed far enough in any one direction, you would fall off the edge of the world.

All that wonderful nothingness, Alex mused, and felt himself tumbling down, down, into the sweet oblivion of sleep.

'Alex,' came an angry voice, and someone was shaking his shoulders roughly, dragging him back to consciousness.

Reluctantly, he opened his eyes.

'What time is it?'

'Twenty-past-three.'

Alex groaned – all he could think of was his wonderfully warm, snug bed with its soft pillows and thick, downy duvet. He'd give anything to be all tucked up.

'Soon be there,' said Fiona, 'I can see lights.'

'Don't,' he said, 'I'm too tired.'

'I can,' his sister insisted.

Alex remained sceptical but looked up anyway. To his surprise, he discovered that Fiona hadn't been teasing him after all. From the centre of the darkness, the distant light-house flashed its non-stop warning to passing ships. To the left was the creamy glow of a small town.

'See,' she said triumphantly.

'Still going to take us ages to get there,' Alex muttered.

It wasn't only the tiredness that was bothering him – ever since leaving Skye, he had been feeling distinctly queasy. It was only by concentrating hard on abstract matters like his thirteen-times-table; French *er*, *ir*, and *re* verbs; and all this century's FA Cup winners, that he had avoided being sick. Fiona hadn't helped. Finding a half-eaten packet of cheese and onion crisps in her anorak pocket, she had taken malicious delight in breathing the pungent smell into his face.

'You're going a bit green,' she said gleefully. 'I saw a bucket in the kitchen. Do you want me to fetch it for you?'

'Leave me be,' Alex said, shoving his tormentor away.

Knowing that the end of the trip was in sight made everything more bearable. Both of them were filled with a sudden rush of energy, and Alex sighed happily as the feelings of nausea subsided. Everything is bearable if you know it is coming to an end: it is the fear that it might continue for ever that makes an unpleasant situation intolerable. That is what is so terrifying about nightmares. Lost in the middle of them, there is no time, no logic, no way out.

As they reached the shelter of the harbour, the violent pitching of the boat instantly ceased. The water was like a mill-pond, and Fiona and Alex looked through the windows at the double row of twinkling lights strung out along the sea-front: reality and reflection. It was only common sense and past experience that dictated which was which.

The immense relief the two children felt on their arrival soon disappeared. True, they had made it across the sea in one piece, but the sound of McCrory's booming voice reminded them of the awful predicament they were still in.

'There they are,' McCrory was saying, 'the three stone dogs.'

'That's why the town's called Lochmaddy,' said Dougie.

'Aye,' said McCrory, 'loch of the dog.'

Fiona and Alex peered out as the boat chugged past the three basalt islets at the entrance to the harbour. They did indeed resemble dogs, as if they had been set there to guard against unwelcome intruders. The children had been to Uist twice before, on family holidays.

'Do you remember those other rocks — what were they called?' Fiona asked.

'*Na Fir Bhreige* — The False Men,' Alex said. 'Of course I do.'

There were two different traditions surrounding the origins of the standing stones. Some said that they marked the graves of three spies who were buried alive for their treachery; some said that they were three men from Skye who were turned to stone by a witch as a punishment for abandoning their wives. Alex believed the story of the spies, Fiona liked the idea of the witch, and the two of them had bickered and quarrelled in the back of the car until Mr McKintosh had finally lost his patience and shouted at them both to be silent.

Alex couldn't help wishing that his father was here now. Even though he was a bit grumpy sometimes, he was brilliant in tricky situations. 'Dad would know what to do,' he said.

'Well, he's not here, is he?' Fiona said. 'This is an adventure, Alex. Why don't you try and enjoy it?'

'I *am* trying,' he mumbled miserably.

'Then try harder!' she snapped.

The old tyres hanging down the side of the *Ben-Davy* cushioned the impact as the little boat knocked into the side of the jetty. The children watched as Dougie jumped off and secured the ropes. They heard the sound of the local fishermen emptying their night's catch into baskets, and smelt the tangy odour of fish and seaweed.

'I'm going to get a couple hours' kip,' McCrory was saying. 'Wake me at ten,' he added, as he unlocked the back door of the caravan.

'Will do,' Dougie called back.

At the sound of the key turning, Alex and Fiona were galvanized into action. They raced into the back room and jumped into the chest where they'd hidden earlier.

'We'll sneak out when he's asleep,' Fiona whispered.

'Shhh! What's he doing?'

The pair of them listened as carefully as they could to Rory McCrory's movements. It was difficult to tell what he was up to. The series of clicks, creaks, rattles and thuds offered no clue. Fiona cautiously pushed the lid open and peered through the narrow gap.

'He's putting the screen up,' she announced.

'He said he was going to bed, not watch a film,' Alex said.

'I don't think he *is* going to watch a film. He's not bothering with the projector.'

'Why's the screen up then?'

'*I* don't know. I'm just telling you what he's doing.'

Alex fell silent, and at that moment they heard McCrory entering the small back room. He pulled a handle in the wall opposite the chest and a foldaway bed appeared. The man sat down heavily and breathed a deep sigh.

'What a night,' he muttered and proceeded to unlace his boots. The children heard them bang against the back wall and clatter to the floor. "'S better,' he said, massaging his aching feet.

A tremor of icy shivers ran the length of Fiona's spine as she suddenly realized where they were hiding. She hadn't given the contents of the chest much thought when she'd climbed in. Now it occurred to her what the soft materials under her hands and knees must be: blankets, sheets and pillows. With McCrory getting ready for a nap, they could not have chosen a worse possible place to hide.

McCrory opened the bed-chest and sleepily reached inside. The shock of touching neither wool nor cotton, but the warm, soft skin of a living being made him leap back. The lid slammed shut. He sat back on the bed and stared intently in front of him: either the rays from the Trauma-scope were getting to him, or there were a couple of children in his room.

'Right, out of there you two,' he yelled, deciding the second possibility was the more likely.

Nothing happened. His surprise was rapidly turning to anger.

'I am not joking,' he roared.

Like a slow-motion jack-in-the-box, the lid opened, milli-metre by millimetre, and two heads emerged. A boy and a girl. They stared at him, eyes wide and mouths agape, resembling nothing so much as two fledgelings in the nest, waiting for the next worm from their returning parents. The sight of the two dishevelled youngsters was so comical that it was all McCrory could do to stop himself roaring with laughter. It was too serious a matter for jocularity, however. McCrory was determined not to make light of it.

'Stowaways,' he bellowed.

The children visibly recoiled. The boy looked as though he was about to burst into tears.

'And you know what happens to stowaways!'

'Hostages, you mean,' the girl shouted back, her green eyes flashing defiantly.

'Hostages?' McCrory repeated, taken aback. 'How do you make that out?'

'You knew we were here. You locked us in deliberately,' she continued. 'You kidnapped us.'

'I did not kidnap you,' he said. 'I had no idea . . .'

'Then why *did* you lock the back door?'

'Because the catch is broken. It would have banged all night in that storm.'

Fiona stared at him. The explanation sounded plausible enough — she had noticed that the door wouldn't close properly. But no, it wasn't good enough.

'Where's Jamie?' she demanded to know.

'Who on earth's Jamie?'

'You know,' she persisted, determined to call his bluff.

'I *don't* know.'

'At the picture show. One minute he was sitting next to us, and the next minute he'd gone.'

McCrory bit the inside of his mouth. His piercing blue eyes softened slightly. It was the booze that had fuelled his rage, he realized — whisky and claret was such an evil mix. The kids' best friend had disappeared: they had every right to feel concerned.

'Jamie, was it?' he said quietly.

'So you *did* know,' Fiona proclaimed victoriously.

'No, I . . . that is . . .' McCrory blustered. 'I mean, I didn't know his name, but I . . . You deserve an explanation,' he said. 'Why don't you climb out of that chest and I'll make us all a coffee.'

'We don't want any coffee,' said Fiona.

'Well, I do,' said McCrory. 'I've been up all night and I'm just about ready to pass out. So if you don't mind.' And he stood up and padded off to the kitchen to put some water on to boil.

'We could make a run for it now,' Alex said.

'Don't be so stupid,' said Fiona. 'He does know something about Jamie and I, for one, am not leaving until I find out what.'

They went through into the main room and sat down on one of the sofas. The smell of freshly ground coffee beans filled the caravan.

'What do they call you, anyway?' McCrory asked.

'Fiona and Alex.'

'Nice names,' he said. 'Still not too late to change your mind about the coffee.'

Fiona turned to Alex: he looked tired out.

'All right,' she said.

'And something to eat? You must be starving – how about a bacon sandwich?'

Alex nodded enthusiastically.

'That would be very nice, thank you,' Fiona said primly. 'Though don't think bribery's going to get you anywhere,' she muttered under her breath, and sat there planning exactly what she would say to McCrory when he got back.

In the event, none of her trick questions or double bluffs was necessary: Rory McCrory had evidently decided to come clean. And as he continued, the explanation became so bizarre that Fiona knew he wasn't trying to keep anything hidden.

'Haven't you ever wondered why the Real-to-Reel Picture Show is still so popular?' McCrory was saying. 'I mean, twenty years ago perhaps, when no one had a video. But when children nowadays can get hold of all the 'nasties' they want, why should they still come along to my show? Why did *you* come?' he asked, looking from Fiona to Alex.

'It's really scary,' he said.

'And you like being scared?'

'Sometimes,' Alex said, and turned away bashfully.

'It's OK,' said McCrory. 'Everyone likes being scared sometimes. But do you know *why* it's so frightening? Do you know what you're watching?'

Both children shook their heads slowly, and McCrory explained all about the Traumascope and the way it finds children's deepest, darkest nightmares and projects them on to the screen.

'And they never have the nightmare again,' Alex repeated, wishing that he had seen his own recurring dream. He could never remember it properly, but he knew it involved lots of faces, laughing at him. Time after time, he would wake up in tears. It was horrible.

'Never again,' McCrory confirmed. 'But — and it's become a big but — very, very occasionally, something goes wrong.'

Fiona felt the hairs at the back of her neck stand up. She shuddered involuntarily.

'Sometimes . . .' McCrory continued, stroking his beard thoughtfully, 'sometimes, the memory is so painful that the dream it causes becomes confused, becomes reversed. And when the Traumascope finds the nightmare then . . . well, the brain refuses to let go and . . . Oh, it's so hard to explain,' he said, and looked down at the floor.

The children remained motionless, waiting for the man to carry on. Both of them felt uneasy. Although convinced now that McCrory hadn't done anything to Jamie directly, he seemed to be suggesting that something even more serious had taken place.

'You see,' he said at length, 'the Traumascope is infinitely more powerful than the human mind. Given a tussle between the two, there can be only one outcome. Usually the projection of the nightmare on the screen is sufficient for it to be cured. But if the brain refuses to let the memory go, then the Traumascope takes the whole person through the screen, so he or she can confront the nightmare — in the flesh, so to speak.'

'And that's what's happened to Jamie?' Fiona asked.

'That would be my guess.'

'I bet you it'll be something to do with water,' she said thoughtfully. 'He's terrified of the stuff, isn't he?'

Her brother nodded.

'So where is he exactly?' Fiona said, turning back to Mc-Crory.

'Behind the screen. No, *in* the screen.'

'Which?' she demanded.

'Neither, really,' McCrory admitted. 'You see, the screen is a sort of doorway into the Land of Perpetual Dreams. That's where they're all stored. That's where Jamie is now, trying to discover the truth of his own nightmare. And that's why I've put it up – to open the door for his return.'

'I still don't get it,' Alex said slowly. 'What do you mean, "reversed"?'

'"Reversed"?'

'You said that the memory which causes the nightmare gets all confused and becomes reversed.'

McCrory nodded. 'The after-image. I'll try and explain,' he said, and went over to the shelf containing his collection of cinema mementoes.

'What's that?' Alex asked suspiciously, as McCrory returned with a copper and glass instrument in his hand. He hadn't forgotten the hypnotic effect of the juggling clown, or the numbing power of the stroboscope.

'It's just a torch,' he said and switched it on.

'I'll look at it first,' Alex told his sister. 'You can have a go if I'm all right.'

McCrory smiled at the boy's mistrust – he could hardly blame him. He shone the dazzling, emerald light into Alex's eyes for fifteen seconds.

'Now look at the screen,' McCrory instructed.

'Yeah,' said Alex, unimpressed.

'What can you see?'

'A large pink blob.'

'And what colour was the light?'

'Green,' said Alex slowly.

'You see,' said McCrory. 'The after-image. You saw green; you know it was green, but your brain has recorded pink. And it's like that with memories. A particular event can be so distressing that the brain refuses to remember it properly – it distorts and twists and sometimes tries to bury the memory completely. But it's not possible. Everything that has ever happened to you since birth – perhaps before – it's all up there somewhere,' he said, and tapped his temple.

'And Jamie?'

McCrory sighed. 'I imagine your poor friend has a difficult time ahead of him. Something must have happened to him in the past. Something terrible. Something that he's denied for years that he'll have to face up to now. We can only hope that he comes to no harm.'

'You mean it could be dangerous.'

'Facing nightmares? Unbelievably dangerous.'

'But they can't really harm you,' Fiona argued.

'Not if you can wake up from them.'

Both children looked down, and McCrory could see they were becoming more and more anxious. He wanted to reassure them that Jamie would be fine, but the memory of Elizabeth McNulty still haunted him. 2 June 1971 – he would never forget the date when he had seen the little girl apparently disintegrate in the light of the Traumascope and get sucked down into the screen. All those years ago and she had never returned. How could he encourage Alex and Fiona that their friend was safe, when he couldn't even be sure himself?

'Will he be there on his own?' Fiona asked finally.

McCrory gulped. 'The Land of Perpetual Dreams used to

be so popular,' he finally answered, avoiding her question. 'Plato, Sophocles and Aristotle; Petrarch, Plutarch and Julius Caesar – they all knew the significance of dreams. And take the Bible,' he went on. '"And Joseph dreamed a dream, and he told it his brethren: and they hated him." Genesis: 37, verse 5. Now *he* could have told you a thing or two about the Land of Perpetual Dreams.'

Fiona remained quiet. She remembered the stories about Joseph from scripture lessons. There was the one about the sun, the moon and the eleven stars all bowing down; there was the tale of the butler and his grapes, the baker and his cakes; and then there was the dream of the Pharaoh himself and how he had demanded to know the meaning of the fat and thin cows, of the good and bad ears of corn. What Fiona had never asked herself, however, was *how* Joseph had made his interpretations.

'You see, he understood dreams,' McCrory explained, 'and he lived at a time when men and women took all that they found in sleep as seriously as what they saw when awake. But it all changed,' he added slowly.

'Why?' asked Alex.

'The Dark Ages,' McCrory said. 'The alchemists spent all their time trying to turn lead to gold – searching for material reward, you understand. They neglected the spiritual side of life. People denied anything they couldn't see or hear or touch – and the doors to the Land of Perpetual Dreams were slammed shut. Until, with my Traumascope, I found a way in once again,' he said proudly. 'But it must be a lonely place today,' he added, and shook his head sadly.

'So there's no one there to help him,' Alex mumbled, relieved that it was Jamie and not he who had been dragged into the curious land.

McCrory looked away guiltily.

'Is there someone?' Fiona asked, noticing the man's discomfort.

He realized that there was little point in concealing any-thing he knew. The children had a right to know, and he told them all about Elizabeth McNulty.

'That's over twenty years ago!' Fiona exclaimed.

'I told you it could be dangerous,' McCrory murmured.

There was a moment of absolute silence in the caravan as Rory McCrory's words sank in. They might never see Jamie again.

It made no sense. Suddenly, both Fiona and Alex were clamouring for more information.

'Can't we contact him somehow?'

'Couldn't we go in and find him?'

'If the screen's up, why can't he just come back?'

'And why should it take so long?'

'Whoa, whoa, whoa,' said McCrory. 'I know it's all a bit hard to take in. Believe me, there's a lot about how the Traumascope works that I don't understand myself.'

'Then why are you playing around with something so dangerous?' Fiona said sharply.

McCrory looked at the angry little girl in front of him. How could he answer her? This was a question he had asked himself so many times already. He had always prided himself on being a healer, but did all the children he had helped justify the loss of Elizabeth and Jamie?

'We're all very tired,' he said finally. 'Things will look a lot different after a sleep.'

I doubt it, Alex thought.

'You two can have the bunk-beds next to the kitchen,' he continued, not allowing the children time to register their objections. 'I'll show you exactly how the Traumascope works later — perhaps there is a way . . .'

'Why not now?' Fiona demanded, as McCrory stood up.

'We'll be able to plan our strategy much better when our heads are a bit clearer. My sons used to sleep here,' he said, turning back the duvets and plumping up the pillows.

'And where are they now?' asked Fiona.

McCrory laughed. 'Well, certainly not in the Land of Perpetual Dreams. No, they grew up and settled down,' he said. 'As adults, they didn't think much of a life on the road — one's a bank clerk and the other's an estate agent. Ben and Davy: I called the boat after them. I like to think that, in a way, they're still with me.' He sighed. 'They didn't think much of the Traumascope either — but then nobody over the age of fourteen does,' he added thoughtfully.

'But . . .' Fiona persisted.

'No,' said McCrory firmly. 'I've made my decision.'

The children could see that Rory McCrory had made up his mind and, remembering how stubborn he'd been with Dougie about the crossing, they realized it was pointless trying to change it. And he was right, anyway. They were both far too tired to think logically.

'I'll wake you in a couple of hours,' said McCrory, and left them to decide who had the top bunk.

Sleep evaded Rory McCrory as he lay on his own bed, arms folded behind his head. He tried counting sheep, but before he reached twenty, the little woolly heads had been replaced by the faces of Elizabeth McNulty and Jamie Mac-Donald as, time after time, they jumped, not over a gate, but through a screen and into the unknown.

'Take care,' he whispered. 'And come back safely.'

—6—
DREAMBOUND

Nightmares are unpredictable creatures. They cannot be controlled; will not be tamed. They are like temperamental horses. Ninety-nine times out of a hundred, they will walk, trot and canter obediently but, when you least expect it, they will suddenly reassert their true wildness. For no discernible reason, the animal will snort furiously, rear up with mane flying and hoofs pummelling the air, and hurl its rider from the saddle. It is impossible to determine how your ride will end.

So it is with nightmares.

Some people try to prepare themselves for the night. They drift off to sleep, whispering the words of someone or something they want to dream about. Others concentrate on avoiding the spooks and demons which threaten to fill their unconscious hours. Both ways are to no avail.

Occasionally, it's true, dreamers can rouse themselves from nightmares and drag themselves back to wakefulness. 'But this is only a dream,' they murmur, and the visions fade away obligingly. But there is no guarantee that this will happen.

Jamie, however, was unaware of this. As he walked along the clear plastic pavement, he reassured himself that there was no real danger, that everything would be all right.

'If I end up in something unfamiliar and dangerous, I know what I have to say,' he muttered, remembering his experience with the Rottweiler. "This is not my nightmare" – and it'll all disappear. Easy as that.'

But the boy was wrong. Nightmares are not logical and the fact that he had managed to find a way out before did not mean he would succeed a second time. Just as you cannot bring anything back from your dreams, so you cannot take anything with you. The moment Jamie entered the dreams, all memory of his forward planning would disappear at once.

Jamie was as prepared as he could ever hope to be. That is, he was not prepared at all. He looked down at the grey and beige pictures below his feet.

He blinked.

Standing on the bank, Jamie looked down into the sluggish water. The river rolled along like molten toffee; thick, slow and viscous – a mere fraction of its usual volume. The parched earth and searing air spoke of drought. It must have been many, many months since rain had last fallen and the shrubs had withered, the grass had disappeared. Dead trees lined the river like battalions of skeletons.

Jamie slithered down the steep, dusty bank on his backside, clutching hold of knobbly roots to slow his descent. At the bottom, he surveyed the scene. It was one of death. The water, far from revitalizing the land it crossed, had poisoned every living thing that drank from it.

With the absolute conviction that comes only in a dream, Jamie knew both what he must and what he must not do. He had to cross to the other side, but he dare not allow any of the water to come into contact with his body. The smallest droplet would prove fatal.

'But how?' he said, looking around.

There were no boats, no rafts, no logs — nothing at all that he could use to reach the other bank and remain dry. As swimming was out of the question, he began to walk along the river, hoping that he would find some means of crossing. Mile after mile after mile after mile he walked, the ferocious sun beating down on his head. His task became more difficult with each successive step and yet, following the imperative of the dream, he never even asked himself why it was so important to get across.

The landscape became increasingly barren. There was nothing between Jamie and the horizon to break the interminable khaki monotony of sand and gravel. The oozing river sliced through the featureless landscape like a festering knife-wound. It was only the occasional mound of bleached bones which indicated that other living creatures had passed this way. Jamie could but pray that their fate would not be his own.

'Where have they all come from?' he said, as the number of skeletons increased. 'And why did they all die?'

Ahead of him, a ragged vulture spiralled down out of the sky. Jamie froze. The scavenger hopped around the fleshless carcass of an antelope, pecking unsuccessfully at the horned skull. The wind and sand had stripped the bones dry. Jamie scarcely dared to breathe as the bird cocked its bald head and looked around for an alternative source of lunch. He *had* to get to the other side of the river. Everything would be all right then. Surely there was some way of getting across.

He scrutinized the river more carefully. And there *was* something. How had he missed it before? A huge round boulder was sticking out of the treacly water a couple of metres from the bank. Another lay a little way beyond that.

And then another, and another. If he could just reach the first one without getting wet, it should be possible to make it right the way to the other side.

He stepped back, carefully counting the paces for his run up.

'A piece of cake,' he muttered encouragingly, but remained unconvinced. The river looked so thick that he knew if he fell in, he'd never be able to climb out again.

'GO!' he yelled, sprinted towards the water and took a flying leap through the air. Alarmed by the echoing shout, the vulture soared off into the distance.

Jamie reached the boulder easily, but as he landed, it had wobbled ominously. Flailing his arms about, he tried desperately to regain his balance. Twice he nearly slipped. But it was all right. He had made it.

And yet something was wrong. At first he wasn't sure what: it was only when he leapt to the adjacent boulder that he realized. The rock was soft.

'But . . .' Jamie said and bent down to inspect it more carefully. Encrusted with dried mud and bits of straw, the rock felt more like . . . but it wasn't possible . . . He leapt to the next boulder and then the next.

The middle of the river. Four boulders down, five to go. And all of them so far had given slightly under his weight when he landed. He looked back. The sight confronting him filled him with an instant knee-trembling, mouth-drying, head-tingling panic. The 'boulders' he had already crossed were no longer lying motionless in the water. They had reared up, revealing themselves as massive hippos with hairy, rounded snouts. The one nearest him raised its head and roared ferociously. Its huge yellow teeth glinted in the dazzling sunlight and Jamie received the full blast of its fetid breath.

'No,' he mumbled.

The mound beneath him began to move. Jamie knew that

if he didn't leap at once the huge animal would rear up, toss him into the air and swallow him whole.

He jumped, and from behind him came the furious crack of those gigantic jaws crashing together. There wasn't a moment to lose. He jumped again. And again. One to go. But, alerted by the noise of the others in the herd, the one remaining hippo separating him from the bank was already beginning to stir. Jamie had no option though. He had to try.

With his heart in his mouth, he sprang to the moving grey mass and, without pausing for a second, made a leap for the bank. The moment he landed, Jamie knew he was safe.

The atmosphere changed as his feet touched the ground. Gone was the searing heat which burnt his nostrils, gone was the rank odour of death. A fresh breeze cooled the back of his neck. He sniffed at the mossy smell of damp earth.

Jamie was in another dream. This was the good news. He felt relieved to have escaped the oppressive drought of the parched African savannah. The bad news was that the lush greenery of his present surroundings was no more familiar. Another WATER (River) dream it clearly was, but this Alpine scene was yet another unknown.

'Hurry up, if you're coming,' came a voice.

'Yeah, get a move on, Peter!'

Jamie turned and saw two boys bobbing around in canoes in the middle of a crystal-clear, but very turbulent, mountain stream. A third canoe was anchored to a rock next to him. Jamie waved, sure that they must have noticed he wasn't who they thought he was.

'Hello, I —'

'Come ON!'

They seemed unaware that he was not their friend Peter.

'Dreams really are weird,' Jamie muttered. 'Especially other people's.'

He looked at the flimsy canoes writhing on the swirling

water and realized he wasn't afraid. In this unfamiliar dream, Jamie found himself longing to do something which, in reality, he would have been too terrified to even contemplate. Without waiting to be asked a third time, he stepped confidently into the tiny rocking boat, picked up the paddle and pushed himself away from the rock.

'At long last,' said one of the boys as Jamie caught them up.

'Sorry, I —'

'Your uncle!' the other exclaimed.

Jamie shrugged. Not only did the boys see him as someone else, they heard him as that person too. It was as though he wasn't there.

'Race you!' one of them yelled and, with his paddle figure-of-eighting rapidly, he sped off downstream.

'Oi, that's not fair,' the other called after him. A moment later, he too was hurtling down the frothing river.

Not wanting to be left behind, Jamie also began paddling. He'd once had a go in a rowing-boat simulator — Mr MacDonald had thought it might encourage his son to try the real thing. But Jamie had never got the hang of the machine. The canoe was different though. For a start, he could see where he was going, and instead of the cumbersome oars that he'd never got the hang of, the paddle was wonderfully manoeuvrable. He was soon racing down through the white, foaming rapids after the others, the blades of his paddle rhythmically dipping into the water — right, left, right, left.

Far ahead, the two boys disappeared from sight as the gradient increased, and the river wound and twisted its way down between vertical rock faces. The roar of the torrent being forced through the narrow gap was deafening. Jamie gasped. It looked so steep, so fast, so rough. But there were no brakes on the tiny canoe: he had no option but to continue.

'Wheeeeee!' he screamed, excited despite himself as he accelerated into the raging current.

He'd never experienced anything as exhilarating as shooting the rapids. Constantly surprised by his own expertise, he would flip the canoe first this way, then that, ensuring that the bow of the boat was always at the front. Time and again he would plunge the paddle into the water to pivot round and avoid an oncoming boulder. The spray of the water stung his eyes. Occasionally the splashback from a rock hit him full on and he was soon soaked to the skin. Down, down, down he careered, faster and faster. And yet, no matter how quickly he paddled, how adeptly he navigated the obstacles, never once did he catch a glimpse of the two boys in front of him.

Gradually, as the river began to level out, the rapids lost their momentum. The boulders he passed were no longer an indistinct smudge, but loomed up one after the other, grey and glistening. And as the surging vitality of the rushing water diminished, Jamie had the curious feeling that the river was ageing. After the reckless speed of youth, it had drifted into a more comfortable middle-age, skirting round the stubborn boulders rather than crashing into them. And now, as Jamie reached the bottom, the river was broadening out and settling down into sedate old age.

It was peaceful now. The only sound was the gentle plash-plash of the paddle breaking the surface. Tall bullrushes speared the still water in the shallows; daisies and dandelions, valerian and loosestrife, splashed the banks with purple, yellow and white. In the distance Jamie saw two old men taking a stroll. There was still no sign of the boys though. Perhaps they, like the river, had aged as they'd descended from the rocky mountains.

Jamie continued downstream. The warm sun occasionally shone down on his shoulders as tiny white clouds scudded across the sky. For a nightmare, it certainly was extremely pleasant — so far.

The faraway sound was no more than a murmur at first. But the volume increased with alarming speed. The murmur rapidly became a mutter, and the mutter a grumble, the grumble a rumble, and the rumble a tumultuous roar. Jamie's heart began to pound furiously. Seeing the river disappear a hundred metres in front of him, it was all too clear what was causing the echoing din. If Jamie was right in thinking that the river had aged as it tumbled down from its craggy source, then who knew what the roaring waterfall might represent?

The journey had become a nightmare after all.

Jamie gripped the paddle with white-knuckled terror as he tried in vain to reach the bank. But the current was far too strong. Even as he paddled upstream, he knew that the edge was looming ever closer; the bellowing thunder made that all too clear. His arms throbbed agonizingly, sweat ran down his forehead, but he couldn't allow himself the luxury of wiping away the stinging saltiness from his eyes.

'Please. Not this,' he muttered. 'Not this.'

The water was merciless. Eddies rocked the tiny canoe and whirlpools set it spinning. Jamie was no longer sure where safety lay: paddling at the wrong time simply accelerated the relentless pull towards the precipice. It was hopeless. Still, the boy fought grimly on.

Just before the drop, the river-bed shallowed out and the water bubbled and boiled, tossing the canoe about like a piece of straw. Refusing to give up, Jamie plunged the paddle down. This final attempt to free himself was to prove his most disastrous; the blade struck a rock and the impact jarred up through the boy's tired arms. His grip slackened for a split second — just long enough for the paddle to be wrenched out of his hands. He watched impassively as the tiny piece of wood drifted out of reach.

Everything had turned to slow-motion. The turbulence was subdued as if the water had turned to oil, and the paddle slipped gracefully over the edge and disappeared. The canoe rotated slightly, so that as it finally reached the edge, Jamie was faced with the view down the waterfall and on to the tiny river, miles below him, snaking its way through the valley. For a fraction of an instant, that seemed to last for ever, time actually stopped.

The canoe hovered: half in the river, half in mid-air. And then the descent began. The cacophany roared all round the boy as his weight disappeared. A final cry of help stuck in his throat.

He closed his eyes and slid down as far as possible into the thin cocoon of the canoe. Falling, falling, falling, and the bottom never arrived. Twisting through the air, Jamie had time enough to think how sad it was that he would never find his own nightmare. He had failed.

As the bow hit the deep pool at the bottom, it sliced through the water like a red-hot poker through butter. Down it plunged, down into the turquoise depths.

I'm still alive, Jamie realized. I'm all right!

He wriggled free of the boat and pushed himself up from the muddy riverbed. Opening his eyes, he saw a shoal of silver fish glittering in the gloom as he aimed for the brightness above his head. But it wasn't until he burst through the surface and gulped in delicious mouthfuls of wonderful air, that Jamie knew he had indeed survived another nightmare thrown up by the Land of Perpetual Dreams.

He knew something else too. The atmosphere confirmed it: golden, jagged, foreboding — and cruelly familiar. There was no doubt.

The search for his own nightmare was over.

*

Back on the bank, he looked around. Everything was as it should be; as it had always been. He saw the weeping willow in the distance and toddled over towards it. Yes, toddled. For if he had been Peter to the boys in the previous dream, then now he had become the three-year-old of his own nightmare.

'Over here, Jamie,' came a voice he remembered. 'Don't wander off.'

It was his mother and he ran towards her, arms outstretched for the comforting cuddle that always followed his solitary explorations. Jamie looked down at his hands. They looked curiously small, but he knew that this was how they always looked in the dream.

'Been foraging, have we?' his dad asked, and Jamie chuckled – not knowing what foraging meant, but recognizing the cheerful tone in his father's voice.

'Found a green stone,' he said, holding it up proudly for his parents' eager inspection.

'That's lovely, darling,' his mother said, and Jamie wondered precisely when this pretty young woman had been replaced by the sullen knitting-machine which now permanently occupied the sofa.

'Right,' his dad said, clapping his hands together, 'let's have a photo. Moira, come and join us,' he called to the girl sitting in the fork of the crooked willow.

Continuing to mouth the lyrics of the song on her radio, she made no move.

'Moira,' Mr MacDonald snapped.

'All right,' she said sullenly and muttered something under her breath.

'I don't know what's the matter with that girl,' Mr Mac-Donald said. 'Little brat – she's never happy.'

'Leave her be,' his wife said. 'It's her age. Adolescence is no laughing matter . . .'

'Evidently,' he replied. 'I hope you're not going to be so

moody,' he said to Jamie, whisking him up off his feet and swinging him through the air.

Jamie giggled. His dad and sister always seemed to be arguing about something recently. She would talk to her brother sometimes, confide in him – but he didn't really understand. Twelve years was far too big an age gap. All he knew was that he liked aeroplane rides when they grabbed hold of one arm, one leg and whirled him round and round till he was hopelessly dizzy – and it really didn't matter which one of them did it to him.

His mum returned with Moira and the two of them sat down next to him on the picnic blanket. His dad lay down on the ground, aligned the camera and set the automatic device whirring. Then he raced over to the blanket and knelt down behind them.

'Smile,' he said.

Moira remained stony-faced.

'Is the flasher on?' Jamie asked.

'Chance would be a fine thing,' Moira said, and all three of them burst out laughing at the little boy's mistake. Not knowing what he had said to amuse them, Jamie laughed too. He liked it when everyone was happy. He held up his beautiful green stone, the camera clicked, and the whole family was captured, grinning into the lens.

It was a warm afternoon and, having packed up the hamper, Mr and Mrs MacDonald lay back on the blanket to sunbathe and 'let their lunch settle'. Summer that year had been awful and the brief period of sun September had brought was very welcome. His dad was soon snoring.

'Can I play with my boat?' Jamie asked.

'Course you can, darling,' his mum said drowsily. 'Moira, keep an eye on him, will you?'

'OK,' she said, taking him by the hand. 'Come on then. Where is your boat?'

'Tied up,' he said, and they walked back to the water's edge, where the toy yacht had been secured to a piece of exposed root.

Jamie sat down on the bank and let his legs dangle in the water; Moira climbed back into the tree and switched her radio back on. Although it was early, the sun had already sunk low in the sky. Everything looked curiously yellow. A gentle breeze blew.

'Can I climb up?' Jamie asked.

'I don't think so,' she said. 'It's a bit too dangerous — don't want you falling in the water.'

Jamie didn't argue: Moira knew best. Sometimes his parents told him to do something for no reason other than 'because I say so', but his sister was more logical, more consistent. If she said it was too dangerous, then it was. He turned his attention to the yacht. With one end of the string wrapped round his wrist, he let the little boat drift out on the current. The breeze made the sail billow just like a real one. When the string became taut, he pulled it slowly back towards him, mimicking the sound of a whistling wind with his lips. He looked up again.

'What's that song?' he asked. 'You keep playing it at home.'

' "Do You Really Want to Hurt Me?" ' she said. 'It's brilliant.'

'Funny words,' Jamie said.

'They're beautiful,' she said and smiled.

Jamie stared at her. Sometimes he didn't understand her at all: he hated being hurt. He turned back to the yacht. A gust of wind had tipped it on its side and the sail was lying in the water. He yanked it back to the bank and tried to dry the white cloth as best he could on his shorts. Back in the water, the little boat sailed off again, fast and straight.

It was only when it passed the leafy branches hanging

down in the water that Jamie remembered he'd untied it. Dragging the now useless piece of string behind it, the yacht was making for the middle of the river where the current was stronger.

'Come back,' he shouted, jumped into the shallow water and began wading after the boat.

'Hey, what are you doing?' Moira said, looking down.

'My boat's gone.'

'Stay where you are. I'll get it,' she said and lowered herself down into the river.

'Hurry up,' Jamie insisted. 'It's getting away.'

'OK, OK,' Moira called back. 'I'm going as fast as I can.'

She strode out into the deep water. Over her knees it went, up past her thighs, until her shorts were wet at the bottom.

'Nearly there,' she said, making a lunge for the piece of string. 'Got i . . . Blast!' she said, as it slipped out of her grasp and the yacht moved on a little further.

Jamie stood in the shallows, his little fists nervously clenching and unclenching as the determined vessel continued to evade Moira's rescuing fingers. The water was up to her chest now and the lilac vest was soaked through. She pushed herself off the bottom and began swimming with wild, splashing overarm strokes towards the boat.

'Come on, come on,' Jamie urged her quietly.

But Moira was not a strong swimmer. Her arms and legs were flailing awkwardly. She hardly seemed to be getting anywhere. The splashing became more frenzied. Suddenly Jamie realized that she wasn't swimming at all: she was desperately trying to keep her head above water. The twisting current had wrapped the underwater weeds around her ankles and they were pulling her down. She disappeared, and Jamie stared in silent horror at the empty river.

Ten seconds past. Twenty. Then, all at once, her head

broke through the surface. She choked and spluttered, frantically trying to breathe, trying to free herself from the treacherous weeds. Jamie stared, motionless, petrified. If this was a teasy joke, he didn't like it. For an instant that seemed to last for a thousand years, their eyes met. He saw the wild, terrified expression begging for help. She tried to call out, but the water filled her mouth, turning a scream to a pitiful gurgle. She went down again.

This time the surface of the river remained smooth.

'MOI-RA!' Jamie screeched, his panic finally finding voice. 'MOI-RA, MOI-RA, MOI-RA!!!'

Roused by the agonized wailing, Jamie's parents dashed down to the edge of the river.

'What's happened?'

'Where's Moira? MOI-RA! MOI-RA!' his mum screamed; her voice echoing Jamie's own hysterical cries.

'No, no, no,' his dad moaned.

The man yanked off shoes and socks and jumped into the water. He waded off towards the spot at which Jamie's outstretched finger was pointing. Soon out of his depth, he dived down into the river, disappearing under the water himself. A few seconds later he resurfaced, only to dive back down again. Over and over he tried: surfacing, diving, surfacing, diving.

It was on his fourth attempt that he found the body. He wrenched the weeds from her legs and pulled it up. Then, with his hand cupped under her chin, he sidestroked towards the bank. When the water became shallow enough, he stood up, gently lifted the limp body and cradled it in his arms. His eyes were red and tears streamed down his cheeks, mixing with the water which had taken her life. The silly, trivial argument over the photograph came back to him: a little brat, he'd called her, when she was just being a typical teenager. How could he have said that? How?

'I'm sorry, I'm sorry,' he sobbed and hugged the cold body tightly to his chest.

Mrs MacDonald stared emotionlessly from the bank. She couldn't shout, she couldn't cry: something inside her had been extinguished when her daughter died. The hurt was so big that if she didn't keep it under control she would fall apart completely. Her son was screaming inconsolably by her side and she knew that she should comfort him, take away his pain. But she couldn't. She simply couldn't.

'Stop crying!' Mr MacDonald shouted at Jamie.

But the boy only bawled all the louder.

'Stop crying!' he repeated, as he climbed out of the water and lay the body down on the grass.

The sight of the pale, waxy skin and blue lips was awful. Jamie opened his mouth and howled.

'STOP IT! STOP IT! STOP IT!!' his father screamed and shook the small boy by the shoulders.

Jamie gasped, and the pain and grief lodged in his throat. He swallowed twice and wiped at his tears with the back of his hand. The angry eyes glaring at him were unfamiliar. Jamie had never seen such hatred in a face before – and it was directed at him. He turned to his mother, but she looked away.

And he knew then that his parents blamed him for his sister's death. It was his fault.

All he wanted was a hug to make the empty trembling go away: all he got was anger and coldness. His father's hands were pinching his shoulders. The strains of 'Do You Really Want to Hurt Me?' continued. Jamie wriggled free and ran off along the bank, sprinting at first in case they tried to catch him up. When it became clear that no one was giving chase, he collapsed under a tree and began to sob uncontrollably.

'They don't care,' he wailed. 'And it wasn't my fault. It

wasn't. Oh, Moira, I didn't mean to do anything. I didn't mean to . . .'

And that was how Jamie's nightmare would end. Every time it recurred the same tragic sequence of events would unfold. Time and time again he had relived that afternoon. With brutal inevitability, the dream would progress from carefree beginning to hideous conclusion. And Jamie would be left; alone with his pain, alone with his guilt. Alone. The three most important people in his young life were suddenly gone. Desolate and frightened, Jamie didn't know what to do with his emotions. He remained below the tree, rolled up in a tight ball, weeping.

He would wake, and the tears would have clogged up his eyes and made his pillow wet. This time was different though. He didn't wake up. As he wasn't asleep, that would have been impossible.

A voice from behind him said: 'But that wasn't what happened.'

He spun round. A girl of maybe twelve or thirteen was standing there; a girl with red hair and milky, freckled skin. She looked concerned.

'What do you mean?' said Jamie.

'Just that,' the girl replied. 'What you just experienced was not what really happened.'

—7—
THE POWER OF THE TRAUMASCOPE

'So, what do you think?' Fiona whispered from the top bunk.

'What about?' Alex whispered back.

'All this stuff about the Traumascope and the Land of Perpetual Dreams. Do you believe him?'

'I don't know. I mean, it's so weird, it just might be true.'

'Odd logic – and why are we whispering? We don't have to go to sleep if we don't want to. Are you tired?'

'Yes,' said Alex. 'But I don't think I *can* sleep. The thing is, why would he tell us such an unbelievable story? He could just as easily have said he had no idea where Jamie is.'

'A double bluff?' Fiona suggested, and sat up with her legs hanging down the side of the bed.

Alex reached out and tickled her feet.

'Get off,' she squealed. 'Try and take this a bit more seriously.'

'Sorry,' he said. 'Look, Jamie isn't here and, I don't know, McCrory seemed genuinely upset – I think he was telling the truth.'

'So do I,' Fiona nodded.

'I'm glad I'm not Jamie anyway,' Alex continued. 'That dream place sounds terrifying.'

'Imagine it though,' Fiona said, 'not only being able to *see* nightmares, but actually to be a part of them . . .'

'I was,' said Alex. 'And it still seems terrifying.'

Fiona jumped back down on to the floor. 'Come on,' she said. 'There are too many unanswered questions. Why didn't he want to show us the Traumascope now? If he can't explain how it works, then maybe he is lying after all. Let's go and look at the thing now — while he's asleep.'

'All right,' said Alex, somewhat reluctantly.

Having pulled their trainers back on, the two children peered cautiously round the edge of the velvet curtain sectioning off the alcove with the bunk beds. It became immediately apparent that their plans had been in vain. They walked into the main area of the caravan.

'Ah, couldn't sleep either?' said McCrory. 'Must have something on your mind,' he added and winked.

He was standing by the long shelf, dusting his collection of cinematographic paraphernalia.

'You could say that,' said Fiona, frowning. Like her brother, McCrory didn't seem to be taking Jamie's predicament seriously enough.

'We couldn't stop thinking about the Traumascope,' Alex said.

'I know the feeling,' said McCrory, laying aside a brass and steel device. 'I've been obsessed with it for years.'

'So how does it work?' Fiona asked.

'Ah, Fiona, what an impatient girl you are,' McCrory said and laughed. 'I'll tell you all I know — but don't interrupt, and don't try and rush me.'

Fiona felt herself blushing and bit her lower lip crossly: it was what her parents were always saying to her.

'You see, the history of the cinema has always fascinated me,' McCrory began. 'It started off with Saturday morning pictures, and then I started sneaking out of the house and going to see whatever film was in town. I lived in Dublin at the time and it cost 1/9d. for a seat in the front row. I always sat at the front,' he added, and grinned boyishly.

'Horror was my favourite. *The Beast With a Million Eyes*; *Attack of the Crab Monsters*; *The Fall of the House of Usher*; *The Blood of Dracula* – I loved them all.'

Fiona shuddered. She was terrified of Dracula, and after one particularly gruesome film, she'd insisted on stringing up garlic all round her room before she'd dare to go to sleep.

'And then science fiction,' McCrory was saying. '*The Quatermass Experiment* and *The Invasion of the Body Snatchers*. Fantastic stuff – really nightmarish!'

'Anyway,' he said, noticing the children growing restless. 'When I grew up, I started collecting all sorts of bits and bobs to do with the cinema: posters, reviews, autographed photographs of the stars – Boris Karloff, Bela Lugosi, Fay Wray – and, of course, these,' he said, indicating the various devices and contraptions on the shelf.

'This was my first,' he said, picking up the Y-shaped object with the disc.

'Oh, I looked at that earlier,' Alex said. 'When you spin it, the man looks as if he's jumping.'

'That's right,' said McCrory, flicking the circular disc and showing it to Fiona. 'See?'

She looked at the little man apparently jumping up and down, and nodded.

'It's called a Thaumascope – not to be confused with my Traumascope,' he said. 'It was one of the first scientific toys invented to show how the after-image works. The human brain is fast, but not fast enough to separate two pictures alternating so rapidly – and so the man appears to jump.'

'And this?' Alex said, touching the machine with the rotating drum.

'Have you tried this one too?' McCrory asked.

A little sheepishly, Alex admitted that he had. The man merely smiled.

'It's a Zoetrope,' he said. 'From the Greek words for life and turning. In English, the Wheel of Life. When you turn the drum and look through the slit, the clown seems to be juggling – as you've no doubt already seen,' he added, and winked.

'There were several other devices invented around the same time,' he continued. 'This one's a Phenakistoscope – it's a bit older, but the principle is the same.'

The children looked through the narrow opening, to see a dog apparently leaping through a hoop.

'*Fenakist*,' said McCrory. 'It means to cheat, or an impostor. A good name, I think. I mean, logically, you know that the pictures are all static, but the persistence of the successive images tricks you into thinking you're watching actual motion. It was invented by a Frenchman called Plateau. And this was Dr Roget's version,' he said, holding up a similar device which showed a trampolinist somersaulting through the air. 'Clever man, Roget,' he said. 'He came up with the first thesaurus as well – you know the kind of dictionary you can use to find words with similar meanings.'

'But I don't see . . .' Fiona began.

McCrory looked at her sternly and raised one eyebrow.

'Sorry,' she said.

'Now, at the same time that these apparatuses were being developed, other scientists were perfecting photography. This,' he said proudly, 'is one of the very first Daguerreotypes.'

'Sounds like a type of dinosaur,' said Fiona.

'Sssh,' said Alex. He wanted to hear about the camera he'd been posing in front of.

'1849, it was made,' McCrory continued. 'Daguerre — another Frenchman — had published a paper on his invention ten years earlier. It wasn't what you'd call instamatic. You needed a silver plate sensitized by iodine for the impression, and then you had to expose it to mercury vapour to develop it. Highly dangerous — but profitable at the time. Daguerrotype portraits were all the rage last century. The breakthrough came when the two ideas came together.'

'The persistence of the image and the individual photographs,' said Alex, wishing that the teachers at his school would make their science lessons as interesting.

'Precisely,' said McCrory. 'And that's what a movie-film is: a series of still photographs which change just fast enough for the human eye to see it as a continuous movement, and the Traumascope,' he added, finally coming to the subject uppermost in Fiona's mind, 'works in exactly the same way. It is no more and no less than a highly sophisticated projector.'

'But you said the Ancient Greeks had them,' Fiona protested. 'And Joseph.'

'I didn't.'

'You did, you said —'

'I said that people then could get into the Land of Perpetual Dreams,' McCrory interrupted. 'The Traumascope is one way in — not the only way.'

'*You* said you wouldn't interrupt,' Alex muttered.

Fiona glared at her brother, but bit her tongue. She'd get her own back later.

'I found an old projector and screen in a junk shop in Paris,' McCrory continued. 'I tried to play normal films on it, but the light flickered so much that it was useless. It didn't matter though — another nice addition to my collection. I discovered the power of the machine by accident. The reel I was using broke and while I was mending it, I discovered that the projector still seemed to be working. The dazzling white of the screen was suddenly replaced with more moving pictures, and, what was more, I recognized them. It was a nightmare I'd had since I was a boy.'

'What was it?' asked Fiona.

McCrory tapped the side of his nose: 'Secret,' he said. 'To this day, I don't know how it works. I have a theory, of course, but I'm not sure how accurate it is. You see, nightmares are like films. The same story is played over and over when you fall asleep. And, just like a reel of film, what you remember is a sequence of individual moments all stuck together to give the illusion of movement.'

Alex closed his eyes to see if what McCrory was saying was true. He thought back to the previous morning when he'd swum out for the bottle that Fiona had seen bobbing about on the sea.

'It *seems* like real movement,' said Alex.

'But it isn't,' said McCrory. 'Any time you want, you can stop and examine one particular aspect of the memory. Just like a still. Close your eyes again.'

Alex did as he was told.

'Now, is the sea actually moving? Is the bottle floating around the way it should?'

'Not really,' Alex admitted and smiled. He could see exactly what McCrory meant. His memory was selective: he wasn't reliving the entire experience, but rather a collage of individual experiences. The shock of the cold water, the way the bottle sometimes disappeared from view, the feel of the glass in his hand.

He looked up at McCrory: 'You're right,' he said. 'Lots of separate bits all stuck together.'

'With a film, if the projector is going at the wrong speed, the image becomes either a sequence of jerky movements or an indistinguishable blur. Well — and this is where the biggest coincidence took place — the faulty light must have been flickering at precisely the same frequency as my dreams. And nightmares,' he added. 'X-rays photograph the inside of your body: the projector was filming the inside of my head, and my broken memories were being displayed on the screen as clearly as any fractured bone.

'And, do you know what?' he said, looking from Fiona to Alex, and back, 'I never had that nightmare again.'

He fell silent.

'Was it a really horrible dream then?' Alex said.

'For me it was,' McCrory said. 'Your own nightmare is always the worst ever. It tormented me all through my childhood. I remember I'd wake up time and again, shaking, sweating, shivering, sobbing — I always went to my parents' room; try and get into bed with them. But my dad would insist I went back to my own room. "But I can't sleep," I'd say. "Count to a million and think of blue," he'd tell me, "guaranteed to get you back to sleep." "Can't I stay here?" I'd plead. "No," he'd reply, and there was no changing his mind.

'So I'd have to go back to my own bed, and if I did manage to get back to sleep again, the nightmare would return. Year after year after year, it went on. And suddenly, the Traumascope had cured me of it.'

'Why *is* it called a Traumascope?' Alex asked.

McCrory grinned: 'Good name, isn't it? It just came to me. You see, the Greek for wound is trauma. And that's what my nightmare was: a wounded memory. And then the German for dream is Traum. So I had the two meanings in one.'

'Clever,' Fiona conceded.

'*I* thought so,' said McCrory. 'And I decided there and then that I would help others troubled with nightmares.

92

Rory McCrory's Real-to-Reel Picture Show was born. I dreamt of travelling around, showing people their nightmares and curing them. The trouble was, for my first show I had over a hundred people in the hall – all waiting expectantly – and nothing happened. Absolutely nothing. It was dreadfully embarrassing – I had to give them all their money back. It was only later that I discovered it only works for children under the age of fourteen.'

'What about you then?' asked Fiona.

McCrory shrugged. 'My wife, bless her, always said I was just a kid,' he grinned sheepishly. 'So anyway, I relaunched the picture show, but with admission limited to children. It worked a treat. Nightmare after nightmare would appear on the screen and then, using strips of real film, I'd give them all happy endings. After all,' he added pompously, 'I am a psychologist, a therapist, a healer.'

'Except for Elizabeth McNulty,' said Fiona. 'And Jamie,' she added quietly.

McCrory looked down at the floor.

'I couldn't guess at that side of the Traumascope,' he said. 'I didn't realize how disturbed some young minds could be.' He turned away.

'You didn't know the screen was a doorway to the Land of Perpetual Dreams,' Fiona said.

McCrory shook his head.

'At least, not the first time,' she continued. 'But you did by the time Jamie disappeared. Didn't you?'

McCrory could feel himself growing angry. How dare this precocious little girl presume to criticize him, a Professor of the University of Life? Who did she think she was anyway? First she and her brother follow him, then they break into his caravan, and now she stands there – calm as you please – finding fault with his brilliant invention. It simply wasn't on.

'Listen,' he said. 'I'll have you know that . . .'

McCrory was not to complete his sentence. He suddenly turned deathly pale and a look of utter terror filled his eyes. Staring straight through the children at some hideous vision behind them, he began to tremble uncontrollably.

'It's not possible,' he mumbled. 'It can't be happening. Not again. Not now.'

'What is it?' Fiona asked, her voice barely audible above the whirring hum of the Traumascope. 'What can you s . . . Aaaaagghh!!!' she screamed, as the black-cloaked figure from her own worst nightmare loomed above her.

She spun round, only to be confronted with the focus of Rory McCrory's continued attention. The entire side of the caravan had been enveloped in roaring, orange flames. Ripping through the sofa, racing up the velvet curtains, they were devouring every combustible object in their path and sending coils of choking, black smoke corkscrewing up towards the ceiling. The carved statuettes in the corners glared defiantly before they too succumbed to the blaze and burned along with the rest. A loud crack echoed round the room as one of the windows shattered in the intense heat.

'I didn't . . . I didn't mean to,' Alex whimpered. 'I'm sorry, I . . .'

While Rory McCrory was detailing the workings of the Traumascope, Alex had been fiddling absentmindedly with the machine itself. Without even realizing it, he had pressed the switch and the Traumascope had instantly whirred into action. 'I'm sorry . . .'

'Sorry?' McCrory repeated. 'Do you realize what you've done?'

As the sea of jeering faces appeared in front of him, Alex realized only too well. By turning the Traumascope on, he'd unleashed its awesome power in a room far too small for the three occupants to cope with. Worse than that, because the beam of light had not been directed at the screen it was whirling round, totally out of control. He, Fiona and Mc-Crory himself were face to face with their most dreaded nightmares. Alex, with his terror of being laughed at; Fiona, battling to escape the bloodthirsty Vampire and McCrory — McCrory, who thought he would never again have to relive his boyhood nightmare — was struggling to escape the crackling, white-hot inferno.

But there was no way out. No escape. The Traumascope had them all in its grip. Cables of light were writhing through the air like furious electric eels, probing deep into the subconscious of the hapless trio and filling the room with their darkest fears.

'Turn it off,' Fiona wailed.

Bats with snarling faces and razor teeth were darting and diving at her. She could hear their demented squealing as they became entangled in her hair, and she clawed at herself, frantically pulling them off. The bats were vile, but they were mere minions. Their master — the tall, caped figure in black with crimson trimmings — stood in the shadows, filing his talon-like nails.

'It's not real. It's all in my imagination,' Fiona attempted to convince herself, hoping that the phantasm might disappear. But it remained. Solid, sinister and with eyes that seemed to bore inside her head.

His skin was deathly pale like wax, his cheekbones high and protruding, his hair black and slicked back. As she continued to stare, the thin lips parted and broke into an evil parody of a smile.

She saw his teeth: the cruel, yellow teeth she recognized from her nightmares. Most were small and even, but two — the canines — were abnormally long and jagged. They glinted in the light of the flames as the Vampire's slug-like tongue licked round them.

If only she could look away. But the piercing black eyes maintained their hypnotic pull and Fiona found herself advancing towards the figure, as in a trance.

'STOP!' Alex screeched, but his sister continued across the room to her encounter with the undead. He grabbed hold of her arm. But it was useless. Fiona had been mesmerized and she neither heard nor felt anything beyond her nightmare.

He turned to McCrory for help, but the man was fully occupied with his own tale of horror. Armed with a wet towel, he was racing round the caravan, beating wildly at the flames. No sooner had he extinguished one part of the fire than something else would spontaneously burst into flames. His task was hopeless — yet he would not, could not, abandon the struggle.

'McCRORY!' Alex yelled. 'HELP!!'

But the man was deaf to Alex's pleas. Like Fiona, he had gone too far into his nightmare to be aware of anything or anyone outside it.

Alex knew he was on his own. He was the only one now who could rescue them all — and even that would be a long shot. Already the mocking faces of his own nightmare were surrounding him; sticking their tongues out, jeering at his pathetic attempts to get to the Traumascope.

He was not a confident boy. In the shadow of his sister ever since she had been born, Alex would be tormented at night by the thought that people were laughing at him. The dream would start innocently enough. He'd be running to receive a pass in a game of football, or standing at the front of the class reading out a story he'd written, when suddenly, the faces of the children around him would change.

'You're hopeless,' one would shout, and a chant would break out.

Hopeless! Hopeless! Hopeless! And Alex would redden:

his knees would tremble and his tongue would glue itself to the roof of his mouth.

'You can't do it,' they'd cry, and none of the words of his story would come out. And the more mistakes he made, the louder the taunting would become.

'You can't do it,' they'd yell, and the football would slip past him on towards the opposing team's brilliant centre-forward.

'YOU CAN'T DO IT!' they yelled now, as Alex tried to get to the Traumascope. 'A miserable wimp like you trying to save the day – don't make us laugh.'

But laugh they did; a sniggering, tittering, ridiculing howl of mirth that echoed round and round the caravan. It obliterated the memory of Fiona's encounter with Count Dracula, it drowned out the sound of McCrory's frantic attempt to extinguish the fire. With his head filled with the nightmare of being mocked, Alex was at the mercy of the dream-machine.

Like all objects of power, the Traumascope must be used with care. Handled wisely it can indeed heal, but in the wrong hands it could cause untold damage. Alex continued to battle on towards the whirring contraption, but in vain. The boys and girls it had dragged from Alex's own night-mare stood in his way, blocked his path. They rushed up to him, one after the other, and poked and prodded him before running off again, squealing with malicious laughter. With every second that passed, Alex felt his resolve diminish. His memory was being drained: he no longer knew why he had to turn the Traumascope off.

If Fiona hadn't screamed, there is every chance that all three of them would have lost their minds. The Trauma-scope's relentless hold on their memories was continuing, turning dream to reality and destroying their ability to tell them apart. His sister's bloodcurdling yowl broke the spell momentarily. He turned to see the Vampire enfolding the young girl in his heavy, velvet cloak and, with gaping mouth displaying his deadly fangs, he stooped down and homed in on her exposed neck.

'NO YOU DON'T!' Alex screeched and, pushing aside the gaggle of children, he hurled himself at the fiend. The head-butt to the solar plexus winded the creature and left him gasping for breath.

'Quick,' he shouted at his sister.

But, despite flapping his hand up and down in her face, Fiona remained entranced.

'If you want a thing doing . . .' Alex muttered and, ignoring the faces that were once again gaining power, he dashed across the caravan to one of the windows.

With one of the human brains asserting its independence, the Traumascope went berserk. Ball-lightning and jagged thunderbolts bounced and ricocheted off the walls; the air was filled with the smell of singeing and the crackle of electric energy. Dazzling silver-white tentacles of light clutched and grabbed at Alex. His determination was such that they merely grazed his scalp. But how long could he keep it up? As Rory McCrory had already noted, given a battle between machine and human, the former was bound to win. Already, both Fiona and McCrory were encased in the blinding cocoon of light. Had the ray been directed at the screen, they would undoubtedly have been sucked into the Land of Perpetual Dreams themselves. As this was not possible, who could say what might happen to them instead?

Alex was at a loss to know what to do. He wiped a clear patch in the condensation with his sleeve and stared helplessly through the window. Life was continuing as normal — out there. The storm had moved on and small grey and white clouds were scudding across the freshly washed sky. Everything looked clean and polished; buffed up by the buffeting wind of the previous night.

On the jetty, the Lochmaddy fishermen had finished sorting out their catch and were sitting on upturned crates, chatting, smoking and mending their nets. They were too far away for Alex to even think of attracting their attention. For them it was just another day, like the day before and the day before that. As Alex glanced over his shoulder at the continuing maelstrom, the contrast between the inside and the outside made him shudder. It was all too immense, too weird. He would have given anything to be one of those old fishermen, drawing on his pipe and nattering about the fish, the nets, the weather: the run of the mill.

But it was pointless wasting his time on wishful thinking. Alex was not a fisherman. He was a twelve-year-old boy trapped inside a caravan with a demented dream-machine and the nightmares it had conjured up. Catching sight of the mocking faces reflected in the glass, he realized that he couldn't hold out against the power of the Traumascope for much longer. In a matter of seconds, it would be too late.

Alex began hammering on the window.

'HELP! HELP!!' he bellowed.

Perhaps the old men would hear after all. He stared at them, willing them, imploring them to take notice. If the wind would just carry his voice over to the jetty . . . But there was no way. The light breeze was blowing in the opposite direction, the old men were too far away — and they were probably deaf anyway.

But having started, Alex couldn't stop. The turmoil in the caravan continued behind him. Fiona's bats were whirling round the room screeching, McCrory's flames were lapping and crackling, the Traumascope continued its dazzling display of lightning bolts, while Alex's own nightmare of mocking faces taunted him mercilessly.

Ring a ring a rose-oh,
Alex is a bozo,
  A wimp oh!
  A wimp oh!
The jerk's in town!

The boys and girls had formed a circle, with Alex in the centre. They were spinning round, their faces blurring together. Time and again, Alex rushed at their joined hands, desperately trying to break free. But he knew it was useless. There could be no escape. The nightmare would carry on to the point it always reached.

They would undress him. They would drag him through muddy puddles and then, waving his clothes in the air, they would run off and leave him. Alone, in the middle of the town square. Naked. And one by one, an inquisitive crowd would assemble around him. No one would help him. No one would say a word. They would simply stand there, staring, as though he were some kind of a freak.

'NO!' Alex yelled. He closed his eyes and clamped his hands over his ears. 'NEVER AGAIN!'

He slipped off his shoe and slammed it against the glass. The window shattered instantly under the impact and jagged fragments flew into the air and glinted in the sunlight as they sprayed up and out, before tumbling back down towards the wooden deck. One piece gashed Alex's thumb. A splinter lodged itself in his cheek.

'Hey! What in heaven's name is going on?' came a voice, and a moment later Dougie Drew was standing there, in his hand the brush he'd been using to scrub away the seaweed thrown up by the previous night's storm.

The skipper, Alex thought. How could I have forgotten?

''n who are you?' Dougie was saying.

'H . . . h . . . help us,' Alex said, struggling to blank out the screaming voices in his head and concentrate on making

himself understood. 'The Tr . . . tr . . . Traumasc . . . the Traumascope. You've got to . . . you've got to turn it off.'

'Do what?' Dougie asked.

'Turn the Traumascope off.'

Dougie hadn't a clue what was going on. Although it
had been his job for the past two decades to ferry Rory
McCrory around the coastline of Britain, he had always
assumed that the picture show was simply a travelling
cinema. And since McCrory knew that no one over the age
of fourteen could properly understand, he had never
bothered to explain otherwise. What was clear to Dougie
Drew now was that the boy at the window – whoever he
might be – was scared half out of his wits. Something was
wrong in the caravan. The man dropped his brush, raced up
the steps and burst into the main room.

Nothing in his life at sea could have prepared him for the
spectacle of utter lunacy which greeted him. He stopped in
his tracks and looked round him. Madmen playing charades,
he thought. There was a girl over by the kitchen, apparently
wrestling with some invisible monster. McCrory was at the
sofa and curtains, beating them with a cloth. The boy was
staring in horror at something in mid-air and moaning un-
happily.

'The Traumascope, the Traumascope, the Traumascope,'
he mumbled, over and over.

'But what is it?' Dougie shouted. Totally unnerved at
being surrounded by this crazy mayhem, his frustration at
not being able to help was turning to anger.

Alex raised his arm.

'The Traumascope.'

He looked to where the boy was pointing. There was one of
McCrory's old projectors, and it was on. Turn the Traumascope
off, the boy had said. Dougie strode across the carpet, flicked
the switch up, and unplugged the machine for good measure.

'Now, will you tell me what's going on?' he yelled.

The machine did not yield its grip on the three minds immediately. Having taken energy from the people themselves, it made no difference at first that the electricity supply had ceased. Only gradually did its power drain away. Fiona's Vampire began to fade and the bats fluttered away to nothingness. The taunting children disappeared, bit by bit, until only their jeering mouths were left. And then, one by one, they too vanished. McCrory found himself swiping at the air with a wet towel.

'It's over,' he said.

Alex collapsed on to the floor and burst into tears.

'It's OK,' said Fiona, rushing over to his side and giving him a hug. 'We're all right now.'

Her brother merely sobbed all the louder. 'I know,' he said, 'I know — but what about Jamie? He can't escape, can he?'

'*He*'ll be fine,' said McCrory firmly. 'It's you that I'm worried about — let's get that thumb bandaged up.'

'How do you know he'll be all right?' Alex persisted stubbornly.

'He's got something he wants to come back to,' McCrory said. 'He's got you, and Fiona. You're his best friends. You are the reason he'll find his way back. But you've got to let him know how much you like him.'

'How?'

'Just think to him. Think of the fun you'll all have once he gets back. Tell him how nice it is having him around. It *will* work. Trust me.'

Alex looked up into McCrory's earnest face. The piercing intensity of his eyes diminished and his curly beard shifted as the man broke into a grin.

'Trust me,' he repeated. 'He'll be back before tonight's performance.'

'You're going ahead?' Fiona asked, amazed. 'After all that's happened.'

'The show must go on,' McCrory said, and laughed. 'The kids here would lynch me if I tried to cancel now.'

Dougie had stood watching for long enough. He'd seen how the three of them had returned to normal some minutes after he'd turned the projector off. He'd listened to them talking about this boy, Jamie. He could remain silent no longer.

'After all *what*'s happened?' he demanded to know.

Fiona tried to explain. She told him about the previous night's show and how their friend had been dragged off into the screen by Rory McCrory's Traumascope. How he was trapped somewhere in the Land of Perpetual Dreams.

'And it's so dangerous there,' she said. 'We know now.'

Dougie remained silent. The girl was quite clearly deranged.

'It's all a bit hard to swallow,' McCrory said to the skipper. 'You see,' he said, turning to the children, 'Dougie Drew is no longer a child. He grew up – unlike yours truly,' he added.

'So you didn't see Count Dracula?' Fiona said.

'Or the horrible boys and girls?' Alex asked.

'All I saw was the three of you thrashing about like people possessed. Never seen anything like it in all my life, and I don't mind telling you I'll be happy if I never do again.'

'Same here,' said Alex quietly.

—8—
JAMIE'S BURIED SECRET

'So what did really happen?' Jamie asked.

'That's for you to find out,' came the reply.

Jamie looked at the girl. The relief of finding that he was not all alone was beginning to turn to irritation.

'Who are you anyway?' he asked abruptly.

'Elizabeth McNulty,' the girl said, laughing at Jamie's impatience. 'And there's no point getting annoyed with me – it's not my fault you're here.'

'I don't even know where "here" is.' he muttered.

'You read the signpost, didn't you?'

'I hardly bothered with it,' Jamie lied. 'I thought it was just another part of the dream.'

'Oh no,' Elizabeth said, 'the Land of Perpetual Dreams is all too real. And you're here because you need to be here.'

'That's what it said on the sign.'

'Ah, so you did read it,' Elizabeth said triumphantly.

'I might have skimmed through it,' Jamie conceded.

'So it was no coincidence you stumbled on your own

dream,' she said. 'You were actually looking for it.'

Jamie nodded. 'But I'm not really sure why. I just followed the instructions.'

So Elizabeth tried to explain. She told Jamie what Mc-Crory had told Alex and Fiona: about the painful memories which the mind distorts, about the after-image of a particularly horrendous event, and about the terrible danger of such a recurring nightmare.

'Unless you confront the truth before your fourteenth birthday,' she said, 'it can never be healed. And you will be haunted by it for the rest of your life.'

'So I have to relive it,' he said glumly.

'I'm afraid you do,' Elizabeth said. 'But don't forget that I'm here.'

Jamie looked at her. How would she be able to help if what he had forgotten was so dreadful? The nightmares he had already endured were disorientating enough — from what she was saying, they had been nothing compared with the horror to come.

'You're from Skye,' Elizabeth said. 'Have you ever been walking in the Cuillin Mountains?'

'Of course,' said Jamie. He and his parents would often drive down south for an afternoon's ramble around the foothills.

'Then you know how dangerous they are.'

'The mist and the compass,' said Jamie.

'Precisely.'

The Cuillins are treacherous. The tumbled jumble of jagged mountains have proved fatal to many a climber, and walkers are little safer. With no warning, impenetrable mists can surround them from one moment to the next, and with all landmarks obliterated, the shortest distance proves difficult to navigate. A compass is useless: the magnetic pull of the rock itself sends the needle skew-whiff and north could be anywhere.

'I'll be your compass,' Elizabeth explained. 'I won't be

able to intervene directly but, if you need me to find your way, I'll be there.'

'And I really have to go through with it?' Jamie asked again.

'I'm afraid you do.'

As they were talking, he and Elizabeth had been walking back along the river bank. The nearer they got to the weeping willow, the more agitated Jamie became. He didn't want to have to experience the nightmare any more. He couldn't.

'You must,' Elizabeth said simply.

Seeing his mother and father on the picnic blanket, Jamie was three years old again. The nightmare had begun. Elizabeth stayed back as the little boy ran over to his parents.

'Can I go and play with my boat?' he asked.

'Course you can, darling,' his mum said drowsily. 'Moira, keep an eye on him, will you?'

'Mm hmm,' came the reluctant response. A younger brother could be a real pain. She hadn't wanted to come on the stupid picnic in the first place.

'Come on then,' Moira said, taking him roughly by the hand. They walked back to the water's edge, where the toy yacht was tied up to a jutting piece of root.

'Now, don't fall in,' she said, and climbed up the tree towards the overhanging fork.

Jamie started to follow her.

'Oi!' Moira snapped.

'Can't I sit up there with you?'

'No, you can't. Play with your boat — that's what you said you wanted to do.'

Jamie sat down on the bank, stung by the tone of his sister's voice. She was always getting at him. His mum would say that it was 'just a phase she's going through', but that didn't make it any better. She was horrible.

He shuddered as his feet hit the cold water, and his dangling legs turned blue. Although it was still early, the sun was already low in the sky, tingeing everything with bitter-lemon yellow. A slight breeze was getting up, turning the air chilly. Jamie inspected the tiny fair hairs on his arm which stood up on pimples of shivering skin.

'It looks like a chicken,' he said.

Moira took no notice. She was deep in concentration, carving into the bark of the tree.

'What's M.M.?' Jamie asked.

'Me, stupid. Moira MacDonald.'

'Oh, yes,' he said, and let the yacht drift out on the current until the string became taut. Then he pulled it slowly back towards him, making the sound of the cold, whistling wind. He looked up again.

'And F.M.?'

'Francis,' she giggled, 'the boy I love.' And she enclosed the initials in a heart.

'With the motor bike?'

'With the motor bike,' she nodded. 'And the leather jacket, and the jet-black hair, and the sapphire eyes.' She looked upwards and sighed.

Jamie stared at his sister in amazement. She was really strange sometimes. He returned his attention to the yacht: a gust of wind had tipped it on its side and the sail was lying in the water. He pulled it in and stood it up again. Moira was holding a cigarette. Time and again she tried to puff out smoke rings through her puckered lips, but the wind dissolved them and whisked them away.

'Ummm, you shouldn't,' said Jamie, horrified at the sight of his sister smoking.

Moira merely smirked.

'I shouldn't do this either,' she said, and swigged at a bottle. Her eyes watered, but she wiped the tears away and grinned down at her brother defiantly. 'Aaaah!' she said, licking her lips.

'What's that?'

'What's that?' Moira mimicked him.

Jamie felt tears coming. She was always picking on him.

'Oh, look at his lip trembling. Don't cwy likkle boy,' she said and laughed.

Jamie knew that it wasn't a very nice laugh.

'Well?' he persisted indignantly. 'What *is* it?'

'Whisky,' she said, suddenly belligerent. 'And if you tell Dad I'll . . . I'll . . . Just don't tell him, that's all.'

Jamie looked at her. She was quite pretty really. Her hair was nice and he liked the vest with the picture on the front. But there was something about the way she was acting that made him feel uneasy. Her movements were all jerky, and her voice sounded different. She kept giggling for no reason.

Absentmindedly, he pulled at the string again, but the yacht refused to budge. He saw that it had wound itself around an overhanging branch, and now no amount of tugging would free it.

'My boat's stuck,' he told his sister.

She ignored him and continued to rock back and forwards to the music.

'*Moi-ra*, my boat's stuck,' he repeated impatiently.

'So?'

Jamie shrugged. She was in one of *those* moods. He lowered himself into the shallow water and waded over towards the stupid boat. The mud squelched between his toes as the water came up to his knees, up to his thighs. He knew his mum wouldn't be happy about him getting his trousers wet, but then if he lost the boat his dad would be cross. If only Moira had helped him. She was muttering to herself angrily, completely unaware of the dilemma her little brother was facing.

'I shouldn't smoke and I shouldn't drink,' she was saying.

'I shouldn't do anything. I shouldn't put on make-up. I shouldn't like Boy George. I shouldn't like Francis McPherson, but I do.'

Jamie trudged on towards the naughty boat.

'I do like him. I love him. And in a couple of months we're going to elope and get married, whether they like it or not.'

Jamie stopped and looked up. He didn't understand 'elope', but he did know what getting married meant. It was what grown-ups did – surely Moira wasn't *that* old.

'You can't,' he said.

'Can't I just?' she replied, and took another mouthful from the bottle. 'You try and stop me.'

'Do You Really Want to Hurt Me?' came on the radio and Moira instantly leant forward to turn it up. She looked away from Jamie and began mouthing the lyrics silently.

'Not that again,' he said. 'You're always playing it.'

'It's beautiful,' said Moira and, after yet another gulp of the whisky, lurched forward to turn the radio up even more. As she moved, the bottle slipped. Despite a vain attempt to grab it, Moira watched the bottle splash down into the river.

'Lucky I put the cap on,' she giggled, as it bobbed about below her.

Wrapping her legs around one of the forked branches, Moira lowered herself, until she was hanging upside down above the water. Clinging on with one arm, she stretched the other down as far as she could. For a second, her fingertips grazed the top of the bottle, but it was just too far away. She couldn't get a firm grip and the whisky floated out of reach.

'Blast!' Moira muttered and swung a little further down. Her only handhold was the stump of a broken branch. She clung on as hard as she could as she lowered herself, millimetre by millimetre.

Willows are fragile trees. Their branches, soft and brittle, are unable to support the weight of a teenage girl. The crack of the wood snapping echoed like a gun-shot. An instant later came the heavy splash of a body hitting the water. Jamie looked on in horror as the river swallowed her up.

A moment later her head broke the surface and she stared at Jamie. Her wild eyes rolled and she cackled with hideous laughter. She swung out haphazardly for the bottle, but it was nowhere near her, and the open palm smacked down on the water loudly.

'Oh, spit,' she yelled and laughed all the louder. 'Jamie,' she spluttered, '*you're* sober. Help us get this da. . .'

Her request was never completed. Water rushed into her mouth and stifled the words. She spluttered and choked and flailed wildly with her arms before being sucked down below the surface.

'Moira,' Jamie said dully.

He looked on in silence as the water near the boat boiled and churned with his sister's frantic efforts to make it up to the air. For an instant it went calm. Then the thrashing began again and for a few seconds Moira's frightened, bedraggled head re-emerged. She stared at him. There was no emotion in the eyes, as if the girl already knew that it was too late.

She disappeared, and the river was calm once more.

'MOI-RA!' Jamie yelled and began wading towards the place where she had vanished as quickly as the treacly water would allow.

'MOI-RA, MOI-RA, MOI-RA!!!' he screeched. So like his recurring nightmare, and yet different. Vitally different.

Mr and Mrs MacDonald were standing on the bank behind him, screaming, shouting and flapping their arms around as wildly as Moira had before she'd been pulled under. Jamie stared at them, bewildered. His father was hurling abuse, but not at the swirling river which had robbed his daughter of her young life, nor at himself or his wife for sleeping when she had needed them most. No, he was shouting at Jamie.

'Look at him. It was his boat. His blasted boat. She was trying to rescue it for him.'

His voice grew higher and louder as the same words were repeated, over and over. Jamie merely stood there, shivering in the cold water, waiting in vain to be hugged. Mrs MacDonald remained silent, but though her tongue was still, her eyes blamed the boy as surely as his father's bitter words. The inappropriately jolly tune continued on the radio: 'Do You Really Want to Hurt Me?'

It wasn't my fault. It was the bottle, he wanted to say. But the words wouldn't come. Moira had warned him not to tell them about the whisky, and though there were voices screeching in his head 'it's not fair, it's not fair', he couldn't betray his sister's trust. Not now — especially not now.

'STOP IT! STOP IT! STOP IT!!' was all he could shout. If only they would stop glaring, if only they would stop hating him.

As if waking from a deep sleep, Mr MacDonald suddenly seemed to see his son for the first time. He waded into the water, picked him up and trudged back to the bank. There was no warmth in the man's grip. Plonked down on the ground like a sack of potatoes, Jamie looked up at his mother. Surely she would bend down and kiss away the pain. But no. As her husband jumped back into the water and made for the spot where Moira's body lay, the woman merely stared out into the river.

'Mummy, Mummy,' Jamie whimpered, and tugged at her skirt.

She might as well have been deaf. She neither answered him, nor looked at him, nor unfolded her arms, which were clasped tight to her body.

Jamie turned to see what she was looking at. There was his dad, resolutely making his way back to them with the limp body cradled in his arms. His mouth was set grimly: his eyes were narrowed. Jamie looked up at his mother again. Staring through her husband, her attention was fixed on something bobbing around in the water under the hanging branches of the weeping willow.

It was the half-empty bottle of whisky. And at that moment, Jamie understood with absolute certainty that the woman knew that he hadn't been to blame for the death. She had noticed all the little changes in her daughter over the previous months and realized that she had entered the rebellious phase so many teenagers have to go through. She knew about Francis McPherson, she knew about the smoking, and the drinking; she knew that Moira had drowned because of her own reckless unhappiness. And yet, by the virtual vow of silence she had taken on that day, she had condemned the boy to suffer alone.

The nightmare was finally over. Jamie was twelve again. He felt the calloused hands which had held him in their stranglehold for years suddenly release their grip. He knew the truth now and would never again be troubled with painful guilt in the cold, dark isolation of night. But it wasn't good enough. He turned to Elizabeth.

'She knew!' he shouted, anger bubbling up to the surface. 'She knew it wasn't my fault. She . . . They . . .'

Jamie didn't know who he felt more wronged by — his father, who had instantly assumed the worst; or his mother, whose silent complicity had ensured that he had erased the true memory of the tragedy and replaced it with a version which had haunted him ever since.

'You mustn't think too badly of them,' Elizabeth said gently.

'But ... but they were wrong,' Jamie shouted. 'They knew they were wrong – they wronged *me!*'

'None of us is ever taught how to cope with loss,' Elizabeth explained. 'It's the hardest thing of all. You live in the same house as someone. Loving them, hating them. Your dad couldn't stand the way Moira was changing. He saw the new men in her life – the boyfriends, the pop stars – and felt her slipping away from him. It's a hard thing to come to terms with. Then, from one moment to the next, she was gone. Can't you imagine how awful he felt: she hadn't wanted to join in with the family photograph and his last words to her were ones of anger. He would never have another chance to make up with her – to tell her how much he loved her.'

Jamie swallowed. 'But it wasn't my fault,' he persisted. 'Why did they have to take it out on me?'

'They didn't mean to,' Elizabeth said. 'They were angry with themselves.'

'They're so horrible all the time,' Jamie muttered.

'How? By keeping you in at night? By not letting you dress as you want? Can't you see what they're doing? They're insulating you from the outside world.'

'But why?' Jamie asked.

'Because they're terrified of losing you.'

Jamie paused. He thought of his father's impatience and his mother's apparent indifference. They certainly had a very odd way of showing their concern. And yet he could almost understand.

When his hamster had died, he'd felt nothing but bitterness after the tears had dried up. How could Smudge have left him? She knew how much Jamie loved playing with her when he'd been sent to his bedroom for the evening. She would run from palm to palm, never suspecting for an instant that the fleshy track was endless. And when Jamie lay in bed, he'd fall asleep to the sound of gnawing and scurrying as the little nocturnal animal played through the hours of darkness. He'd angrily rejected his father's offer of a new pet. Yes, he could understand a little. But that didn't make it any easier to bear.

'And anyway,' he said, as if he'd been talking all the time, 'they're grown-ups. It's not the same.'

'Oh, Jamie,' said Elizabeth, 'if I've learnt one thing being in the Land of Perpetual Dreams, it's that adults are just big children.'

Jamie thought back to the dream of the party in the big house. The little man who had offered him drinks had been no bigger than a child himself. He wondered if that had been a boy's nightmare of never growing up, or a man's dream of remaining a boy.

'Things change outside, sure enough,' Elizabeth was saying. 'You can ride a motor bike at sixteen; vote when you're eighteen. But nothing really changes inside. Everyone's mum and dad is just a great big girl and boy, with the same fears and the same dreams that they ever had. They pretend to be grown up for the sake of their own children. But if something really awful happens, they simply crumple up inside. Just the way you did.'

'You mean there's no difference,' said Jamie. He'd been longing for the day when he could leave home and travel around the world.

'Yes, there is one difference,' Elizabeth said, frowning slightly. 'A child's nightmares can be healed. An adult is stuck with them for ever. That's why you're so lucky, Jamie.'

'Lucky?' he said. Obviously he hadn't explained well enough what it was like spending a wet weekend in the MacDonald residence.

'Yes, lucky,' she said. 'Thanks to Rory McCrory and his

114

travelling picture show, you've been able to sort out your memories in a way no psychologist or psychiatrist ever could. You can go back now. You're better.'

'Back!' Jamie exclaimed. He'd somehow forgotten all about returning to reality. But now Elizabeth had suggested it, the idea suddenly sounded very attractive. He thought of Alex and Fiona, and school football matches, and leaving footprints in the sand, and building snowmen, and Christmas — and his parents. They were certainly a bit odd, but they were all he had — and they weren't *that* bad. Jamie found himself standing there with a big silly grin on his face.

He looked at the girl with the red hair and freckles. Her eyes looked so very, very sad. She smiled weakly.

'You won't forget me, will you?'

Jamie realized that he knew nothing about this Elizabeth McNulty other than her name. She certainly didn't seem like a dream.

'No I'm not,' she replied to his question. 'I came here — like you.'

'What, and you haven't found your nightmare yet?' Jamie asked.

'Oh, I found it all right.'

'And it didn't help?'

'It did what it was supposed to do,' she said cryptically.

'Then why are you still here?'

The girl shrugged and looked away.

'Elizabeth,' Jamie said. He was beginning to feel a bit irritated with her. There were lots of meaningful looks and sighs, but why didn't she just come out and say what was wrong. *He*'d understand if anyone did.

'How long have you been here anyway?'

'I've lost count,' she said, 'but it must be . . . ooh, twenty years or so.'

'Twenty years!' Jamie shrieked and burst out laughing. It

had to be a joke. But a glance at Elizabeth's face was enough to tell that she wasn't trying to be funny.

'You're serious,' he said quietly. 'Twenty years. But . . . I mean, what do you eat?'

It was Elizabeth's turn to laugh. 'You'd be surprised the number of people who dream of food.'

Jamie continued to stare. He didn't know how long he'd been in the Land of Perpetual Dreams, but certainly no more than a couple of days at the very outside. And *he* was ready to go back.

'But why?' he asked.

Elizabeth bit into her lower lip and Jamie could see her eyes brimming with tears.

'What is it?'

'I've no one to go back for,' she snapped. 'No one!'

'Everyone's got someone,' said Jamie, and instantly wished he hadn't.

'Oh, I've got someone. Two someones in fact. Aunt Thomasina and Great-Aunt Grizelda. They've looked after me ever since my parents died. Looked after, huh! That's a joke and a half. They locked me up in the attic of their huge house; wouldn't let me go outside, wouldn't let me go into town, wouldn't let me go to school. Aunt Thomasina used to give me lessons up there: Latin, Greek, philosophy and algebra. That was all. "A logical mind is a godly mind" was her motto. I wasn't allowed to read books, to listen to music, to make friends . . .'

As her tirade had progressed, Elizabeth had talked faster and faster, scarcely even pausing for breath. Suddenly, the words had choked in her throat.

'It sounds awful,' Jamie offered sympathetically.

'You don't know the half of it,' Elizabeth said, and she was off again. 'And the meals. The meals! Seven o'clock, one-thirty and six o'clock, the same sloppy cereal mush and a slice of raw lemon. Can you imagine never looking forward to dinner-time? Every one the same as the one before — and it was disgusting the first time! Great-Aunt Grizelda claimed that it contained every essential mineral to guarantee a long life. And she should have known: she was 103. But what a life! She's just a hideous old bag of bones with stubble you could grate cheese on. And Aunt Thomasina's worse. She looks like a pantomine horse in a tartan skirt and sensible shoes. And what are you smirking at?'

'Nothing,' said Jamie sheepishly.

'Out with it!'

'It's just. Well, they sound like something out of a Roald Dahl book.'

'Ronald who?'

'*Roald* Dahl. He wrote these brilliant books and there's always . . . Oh, it doesn't matter,' he said, realizing that as Elizabeth hadn't been allowed to read books, she would have no idea who or what he was talking about.

'The thing is,' he said slowly, unsure how to phrase his proposal. 'The thing is, you don't have to go back to them, do you? Anyway, I doubt whether even Great-Aunt Grizelda could live to 123, do you?'

'I wouldn't put it past her.'

'You could come and live with us,' he finally managed to blurt out.

'But, Jamie, your parents sound almost as bad!'

'You don't want to listen to everything I say,' he said. 'I get a bit carried away. My dad's . . .' he couldn't think of anything in particular to say. 'And my mum loves knitting!' he added enthusiastically. 'She'd knit you up a cardigan, no sweat.'

Knowing what sort of shapeless beige monstrosity he might be letting Elizabeth in for, Jamie decided to change the subject.

'And there's a room there for you.'

'Moira's room,' she said quietly.

He realized what he was saying. Little more than five minutes after he had seen how his sister had really drowned, he was giving away her room to someone else. But it hadn't been five minutes. Moira had died nine whole years ago. That was how long it had taken him to overcome his misplaced guilt.

'The room should be lived in,' he said simply. 'I hate sleeping next to it now – it's all preserved, like something in a museum. The posters and the stupid fluffy animals. It's horrible.'

'All right, all right, don't go upsetting yourself,' said Elizabeth. 'I'll think about it. Even if I were to agree, your parents might have a different opinion on the matter.'

'They won't, they . . .'

'All right,' she said firmly, and Jamie knew that he shouldn't push it too much.

'How much further is it?' he asked.

'Not far now.'

They'd been walking through the fields behind the river and were approaching what looked like a road. As they drew near, it all disappeared: the ripening barley swishing against their legs; the skylarks hovering, whistling above them; the chilly wind at the back of their necks. Like surfacing on an underground escalator, Jamie and Elizabeth emerged out of the dreamscape on to one of the giant rolls of film. Far ahead of them was the signpost.

'You must know this place like the back of your hand,' said Jamie.

'After twenty years, I should do.'

Neither of them spoke another word as they neared the podium. Elizabeth was weighing up the countless pros and cons of leaving the land which had, in a curious way, become her home. Jamie scarcely knew what to think. It seemed the obvious solution, and yet he had to admit that there was a fairly big chance that his parents would scupper the whole plan. After all, they scarcely even spoke to *him*! But he could hardly tell Elizabeth that her worries might prove well founded, not after getting her hopes up.

Jamie noticed at once that there was something different about the central area. Apart from the signpost and the notice-board, there was now a trap-door. And it was open.

'Where did that come from?' he said.

'It's always there.'

'Wasn't when I was here earlier.'

'Then the screen couldn't have been up.'

'The screen?'

'It's like a door,' said Elizabeth. 'That's the way you came in and that's the way you leave. Down those steps, through the screen and you're back in the normal world.'

'Just like that?'

'Couldn't be easier.'

'So you *are* coming,' Jamie said.

Elizabeth looked over towards the noticeboard. Each and every instruction was so familiar to her. Two or three seemed to stand out. Do not proceed until you are one hundred per cent sure you are heading in the correct direction. *Take care! Any mistakes made at this stage could prove fatal.* REMEMBER: ANYTHING CAN HAPPEN – AND PROBABLY WILL! It applied just as much to the real world as to the Land of Perpetual Dreams, and at least she knew how to get around here.

She looked at Jamie. 'You go. I'm just not ready.'

'Not ready,' he said, 'after twenty years! When will you be ready then?'

'Maybe never.'

'You can't live in dreams for ever.'

'I've been doing all right so far,' she snapped. 'Better than what I left behind, at any rate.'

'All right,' said Jamie calmly.

'All right what?'

'If you're going to stay, then so am I.'

'Oh, good grief! This is ridiculous!' Elizabeth exclaimed. 'You can go back, you want to go back – here's the door. Just go!'

'Not without you,' Jamie said stubbornly.

'You stupid, obstinate little idiot!' Elizabeth yelled. 'What do you want to stay here for? No flowers, no trees, no stars: not real ones anyway. Every time you think you're somewhere pleasant, it turns into the deranged ramblings of yet another nightmare. No pets, no neighbours, no friends, no . . .'

Jamie didn't need to say a word. Elizabeth looked at him and he knew that she'd convinced herself to join him.

'Take my hand,' he said. 'Not that I don't trust you!'

'It's OK,' said Elizabeth and laughed. 'I'm not sure I trust myself.'

Having taken one last look around the curious land, with its countless nightmares radiating out on strips of film, Jamie knew that he for one would not be sorry to leave. The Land of Perpetual Dreams was far too unpredictable.

He went down the rickety steps one at a time. Ahead of him was a large white square.

'That's it,' said Elizabeth.

'Why didn't I come here when I first arrived?' Jamie asked. 'It would have saved a lot of bother,' he added, as the full horror of the slavering Rottweiler came back to him.

'You did, but getting here is so disorientating that you probably wandered off into some dream or other before you'd come round.'

'I did that all right,' he said.

'A bad one, was it?' Elizabeth asked.

Jamie nodded. 'Now what?' he said, as he came right up to the screen.

'Just walk through.'

'You sure?'

'Sure I'm sure,' she said, and Jamie did as he was told.

Elizabeth was right. His right arm and left leg passed through the canvas as though it wasn't there at all. Then his head, and he found himself looking into a whitewashed hall, where three people were arranging collapsible chairs in neat rows. He recognized them.

'Alex,' he called, 'I—'

An unexpected wrench on his left arm jerked him painfully backwards. He turned and yelled at Elizabeth.

'What are you doing?'

'Jamie, I can't,' she said.

'Oh no, not that again. I thought we'd agreed . . .'

'I haven't changed my mind,' she interrupted. 'I just can't,' she said, and tugged at the chain around her neck.

Jamie saw the little heart-shaped gold pendant she was wearing flash and spark; the chain itself was glowing as if white-hot.

'What is it?' he said, suddenly alarmed.

'It's my mother's, she said. 'But it isn't real.'

Jamie passed back through the screen.

'What do you mean, it isn't real?'

'I took it from the nightmare. I'm sorry, Jamie, I'd forgotten — it was so long ago.'

'Bring it with you. One little souvenir won't matter.'

'I can't,' she said irritably. 'Don't you understand? It won't let me. It isn't possible to hold on to a dream in real life.'

'Then take it off.'

'No, I won't!' she snapped.

'And the alternative?'

'I'll have to take it back.'

'What, go back to your dream?'

'I've got to,' Elizabeth sobbed. 'It's hers. I can't just throw it away.'

Jamie sighed. This was one little hitch he hadn't envisaged, and after coming so close to escaping, it was just what he didn't need. But Elizabeth was adamant: that much was clear, and as he'd promised he wouldn't leave the Land of Perpetual Dreams without her, he had no choice but to return.

'This had better be worth it,' he muttered as he tramped up the stairs behind her.

'I'm sorry, Jamie,' she was saying as she hurried up to the signpost. 'I just couldn't . . .'

'It's OK,' he said, resigned to the fact that their ETA in reality would have to be delayed. 'But let's get it over with as quickly as possible. I've just about had my fill of nightmares,' he shuddered.

—9—
THE GOLD LOCKET

'Jamie,' Alex screamed. 'JAMIE!'

But it was already too late. As mysteriously as the fuzzy spectre of his friend had emerged from the screen, so it had disappeared again. Someone or something had dragged him back.

'He was there,' Alex said. 'I'm not making it up. Honest!'

'It's OK,' McCrory said reassuringly. 'We believe you. We heard him, didn't we, Fiona?'

'He called you,' she said to her brother.

'He did, he did,' Alex said excitedly. 'I looked up and there he was, coming through the screen. But ... but ...' he stared at the floor. 'What went wrong?'

'At least we know he's safe,' said McCrory.

'Do we?' Alex said. 'Why did he go back? Something must have gone wrong.'

'I don't know,' McCrory admitted, 'but I'm sure it's all going fine.'

Fiona looked at him closely. Not for the first time, she

felt that Rory McCrory knew more than he was letting on. But, seeing there was nothing they could do, she decided to give him the benefit of the doubt. They would just have to be patient that little bit longer.

'Right,' she said, all business-like. 'Let's get these chairs finished. The doors open in under an hour.'

After a huge brunch of eggs, bacon, fried bread, tomatoes, orange juice, cornflakes, toast, marmalade and Earl Grey tea, McCrory and Dougie Drew had set to work. They undid all the ropes tethering the caravan into place, and led the horse from the rocking *Ben-Davy* and on to the jetty. Then, with Fiona and Alex sitting beside him, McCrory had taken the reins and gee-ed up Major into action. They had clip-clopped along the sea-front and up along the narrow streets towards the town hall. Posters announcing the evening's performance of the Real-to-Reel Picture Show were already up, and a crowd of children was soon running alongside, cheering excitedly. At the hall, McCrory had carried the Traumascope and screen inside, and all four of them had started to put the chairs out in rows.

'But what do you think's happened?' Alex persisted.

'I'm sure Jamie'll tell us when he gets back,' Fiona said, matter-of-factly.

'*If* he gets back,' Alex muttered darkly.

Fiona ignored her brother's dramatic aside and busied herself with the chairs. It was time to look on the bright side.

'Make sure you leave enough leg room,' McCrory called to them. 'Nothing worse than being all cramped up.'

And the air was filled with the sound of scraping wood on wood, as they widened the gaps between rows. It was good doing something mechanical, Fiona thought. It made you forget what might be happening on the other side of the screen.

*

'It's this way,' Elizabeth announced.

'Sure?' said Jamie.

Elizabeth looked at him incredulously. As if *she* wouldn't know where she was going, after all the time she'd spent in the land of dreams.

'Sorry,' said Jamie. 'I just don't want to make any mistakes.'

'Neither do I.'

'CARS (speed),' Jamie said, looking at the way they were heading on the signpost.

'CARS (crash),' Elizabeth said, and spun round. 'We're not . . .'

'Just checking,' he said and grinned.

'Not funny!' she said sternly. 'If it was speed, I wouldn't be here now.'

Elizabeth had mentioned before that her parents had died; it suddenly occurred to Jamie that they were the reason she had been sucked into the Land of Perpetual Dreams. Maybe, like him with Moira, she had blamed herself for their deaths. And from the reel of film they were following, it seemed as though they might have been killed in a car crash. He felt so sorry that he'd distressed her all over again, but he didn't know what to say to make things better.

In the end, it was Elizabeth who spoke first. The plastic road they were walking along had once again swallowed them up, and they found themselves in another dreamscape.

'Haven't been here for a while,' she said.

'I expect it's too upsetting,' said Jamie.

Elizabeth nodded.

Jamie looked around. They were walking along a muddy path on a cold midwinter's morning. Slimy black leaves underfoot made walking difficult; in the distance was the sound of revving engines.

'Is this your nightmare?' he asked.

'No,' came the reply, 'this is all about a racing driver having a crash at Silverstone Race-track. No, we go down here,' she said, and turned down a narrow track through the trees.

'You must have seen some pretty incredible nightmares over the years,' Jamie said.

'You're not kidding,' said Elizabeth.

'What was the weirdest?'

'Well, I remember one which starts off on these red and white squares. I only discovered it was a tablecloth when I caught sight of this huge great jelly heading towards me. It *was*!' she said, seeing the disbelief in Jamie's eyes.

'It had left the plate it was on, and was trundling towards me like a gigantic strawberry-flavoured amoeba. I couldn't believe it — I'd only gone into the dream because I was hungry, and suddenly there was my snack about to eat me!'

'So what did you do?'

'There wasn't much I *could* do. Whichever way I ran I soon came to the edge of the table, and the drop down was like looking over a cliff. I dodged this way and that, and still the jelly kept coming. It made this disgusting slurping noise. Vile! I managed to get out of its way for ages, but finally it cornered me. The smell of rotten strawberries was overpowering. I tried running into it. After all, it's only a jelly, I kept telling myself. But it was solid — in a wobbly sort of way — and I just bounced back off it, lost my footing and keeled over backwards off the edge of the table.'

'And then what happened?'

'It turned into a falling dream,' she said. 'You'd be surprised how many do.'

'What do you think it means?' Jamie asked.

'Insecurity, I think. Especially about the future. From my experience, half the population seems frightened about what's going to happen to them.'

'And the jelly?'

'I don't know. It's difficult to think of anyone being terrified of their pudding, isn't it?'

'My mum's custard can be a bit scary sometimes,' Jamie laughed. 'You never know what might be lurking behind the lumps.'

Jamie liked the story, but it wasn't really what he'd been asking about. True, it was weird, but he wanted to discover the more bizarre fantasies that people had at night. He wanted to hear about the darker side of nightmares. But if Elizabeth knew, she wasn't telling.

'Some people's nightmares are simply too unpleasant,' she said in a hushed voice. 'Cruel, brutal and callous. No one ought to see them,' she added, and turned her head away.

It occurred to Jamie that although Elizabeth was technically still only thirteen, the countless nightmares she had experienced had given her an understanding of human nature far in excess of her years. And clearly she hadn't liked a lot of what she'd seen.

'Moira wasn't as nice as I thought,' he said, changing the subject.

'Your sister?' said Elizabeth. 'She was all right. A typical teenager.'

'But I'd remembered her as kind and understanding. I thought she loved me,' Jamie said.

'She did!' Elizabeth said emphatically. 'That much was obvious.'

'Funny way of showing it,' said Jamie.

'Look, how do you think you'd feel now if you had to spend half your time looking after a three-year-old sister — however sweet?'

Jamie considered the situation. 'A bit miffed, I suppose,' he conceded.

'She was just a normal adolescent coping with growing up,' she said.

There was something a bit know-allish about Elizabeth, Jamie decided. He hoped it wouldn't get on his nerves when – if she *did* come and live with them.

'Everyone idealizes the past,' she added.

'You didn't,' said Jamie, remembering her tales of Aunt Thomasina and Great-Aunt Grizelda.

'Oh, but I did. They were *far* worse than I described,' Elizabeth laughed. 'Not that way!'

Jamie had been wandering off to the left, across a wide grassy expanse covered with daisies, cowslips and clover. Had he been on his own, he would have continued down into a nightmare that Elizabeth said was particularly horrible. A family had driven down to the seaside for the day. As it was too cold for swimming, the father had parked at the top of the cliffs, and they had all eaten their sandwiches and drunk their tea in the car. It was only when they were about to leave that they discovered how slippery the mud was. The rear tyres spun uselessly as they had tried to set off. Instead of accelerating forwards, the car had slipped back to the edge of the cliff, where it had come to rest; half on solid ground, half suspended in mid-air.

'How did it end?' Jamie asked, as Elizabeth's story ground to a halt.

'I didn't wait to find out,' she said, turning down a side-street. 'It's this way. We're nearly there.'

'At long last,' Jamie muttered.

'All things come to he who waits, Jamie,' said Elizabeth.

'That's what my mother says,' he said irritably.

'And patience is a virtue,' she added.

'Elizabeth! Stop being boring.'

'Sorry,' she said. 'Look, you see that building over there – that's where it all starts.'

'Your nightmare?'

Without answering, Elizabeth crossed the main road and

made for the roadside café. Jamie followed. There were several vehicles parked at the front: lorries, vans and a collection of old-fashioned cars. At least, they looked old-fashioned to Jamie.

'That's our one,' she said, pointing to a pale green Morris Minor. 'My parents are in the café.'

Jamie felt shivery tingles of nervous expectation running up and down his spine as they went in. The large room was warm and smoky. It smelt of stewed tea and burnt fat. A skinny woman in a pink nylon housecoat was rushing about, taking orders and delivering endless trayloads of greasy breakfasts to the hungry customers.

Elizabeth left Jamie standing by the counter and walked towards the corner table. A tall man with thinning fair hair and a woman with a ponytail and smiley eyes were sitting there chatting. Mr and Mrs McNulty, Jamie thought. To him, Elizabeth still looked the same, but to the couple in the nightmare, she toddled towards them, their three-year-old daughter.

'Elizabeth!' the woman exclaimed and grinned happily.

'Mummy!' Elizabeth replied and rushed into the outstretched arms. Giggling, the little girl was swept up and plonked down on her mother's lap.

'And who's my favourite little porky-pie?' Mrs McNulty asked, and planted kisses all over Elizabeth's gleeful face and squirming shoulders.

'Me,' she chuckled.

'You, you, you! Careful now, or you'll break it,' she said, as Elizabeth's podgy fingers grasped at the gold heart around her mother's neck and yanked down on the chain.

'Can I see?'

'Gently then,' she said, as she reached behind her neck and undid the clasp. She put it round Elizabeth's neck. 'Here we are.'

The girl looked down and frowned in concentration as she tried to unclip the two halves of the heart. It kept slipping out of her grasp and bouncing back down to her chest.

'You need longer nails,' her mother said, prising the hinged heart open.

Inside each half was a tiny photograph. One of the man, and one of the woman.

'This was Daddy the day we got married,' she said. 'Doesn't he look smart?'

'Had more hair then,' Mr McNulty commented gruffly.

'And this is Mummy. Look, no wrinkles.'

'Hair, hair,' said Elizabeth.

'Yes, I had it black then. Do you like it?'

Elizabeth screwed up her nose and shook her head.

'Neither do I,' her mother laughed.

'I think we should be making a move,' Mr McNulty said. 'Before the traffic gets too heavy.'

'Come on then, pudding,' Mrs McNulty said, and deposited her daughter back on the lino tiles. 'Off we go. Do you want to wear my chain? You'll look after it, won't you?'

The little girl nodded and inspected the shiny gold heart proudly. From his vantage point, Jamie began to panic. Elizabeth couldn't keep it on, otherwise she would never make it back to reality. She *had* to give it back. And he waved his arms in an attempt to get her attention.

'Elizabeth,' he hissed, 'take it off.'

The girl continued to stare at the tiny medallion.

'Take it off!' he repeated more loudly.

She looked up and stared straight through him. Jamie felt his heart racing: surely it wasn't too late already.

'Elizabeth!' he shouted, flapping his hands about wildly.

Her eyes focused on his, but there was no sign of recognition. Then, as he kept watching her face, he saw something register. It was as if she were waking from a trance. She smiled weakly and raised her hands slowly. This time would be different, this time she wouldn't keep the souvenir of the parents she had loved so much. This time, she would free herself from the nightmare.

'Here, Mummy,' she said, and handed the chain to her. 'You wear it.'

'Thank you, darling,' her mother said: she didn't notice the tears streaming down Elizabeth's cheeks.

And as she clipped the chain into place around her own neck and the gold heart disappeared under her blouse, the nightmare ended. Jamie and Elizabeth were suddenly the only two people remaining in the café. Elizabeth hurriedly wiped away the tears on the back of her hand when she noticed Jamie staring at her.

'Silly,' she sniffed. 'After all these years.'

'What happened?' Jamie asked.

'A crash,' Elizabeth said flatly. 'This tractor pulled out of nowhere, Daddy swerved to avoid it and we hit an oncoming lorry. It wasn't my fault, but like you, I blamed myself.

'I remember the fireman who cut me free,' she said thoughtfully. 'He had the greenest eyes I'd ever seen – and he held his jacket up, to shield me from the sight of . . .'

She stopped and Jamie knew better than to interrupt her memories. They walked back through the dreamscape in silence. Through woods, over fields, down narrow alleys and over motorway bridges they walked. Neither said a word, but Jamie and Elizabeth knew that they were both now ready to return to reality.

It was only when the setting for the dreams once more faded away, and they found themselves walking along the plastic road, that Jamie finally dared to speak. He wanted to tell Elizabeth how brave she'd been.

'Well, it took me long enough,' she said.

'Better late than never,' Jamie said and laughed – he could be just as good as Elizabeth at speaking in banal little truisms.

They continued on towards the central podium, and Jamie

looked round at the curious scene. It was so well ordered; so disciplined: the spokes of countless dreams radiating out from the central hub, with its signpost and notice-board. Above, the sky was white and completely characterless, like a wide expanse of unblemished laminate. Whoever had created the Land of Perpetual Dreams, Jamie was suddenly convinced it hadn't been a man or a woman. The dreams, with their dirty corners and sordid secrets, were human, but the land in which they had been stored was not.

'You mean Martians?' said Elizabeth.

'I don't know, but look at it,' Jamie said, sweeping his arm round the geometrical landscape.

'Maybe people in the past were just more logical.'

'Well, I certainly won't miss it. I like a bit of chaos,' said Jamie. 'This is . . . unnatural.'

'You're not wrong there,' she said. 'Come on, let's go if we're going.'

Jamie spun round anxiously. 'Hang on,' he said. 'Where is it?'

'Where's what?'

'The trapdoor,' he snapped, 'its disappeared.'

'All right, don't panic,' said Elizabeth. 'They must have taken the screen down for some reason. I told you that we could only get back when it's up.'

'So what happens if it gets damaged?' Jamie asked, suddenly seeing his entire, endless future in this clinical, laboratory-clean land.

'They mend it, I suppose,' she shrugged.

'And what if someone steals it?'

'Why should anyone steal a screen?'

'And McCrory travels around by boat — what happens if it gets washed overboard and swallowed by a whale, or struck by lightning, or . . . or . . .'

'Calm down, Jamie. None of that is going to happen.'

But Jamie was inconsolable. All at once, the screen had

become the most valuable and fragile object in the world: everyone was after it, and the slightest jolt would rip the linen to shreds.

'Jamie! They're probably just moving it from the caravan to the hall. Just give it ten minutes and I'm sure it'll be back.'

Jamie glared at her, but kept quiet. He knew he was being stupid; he knew that ten minutes more wouldn't make any difference – but there was nothing he could do about his impatience. In the short time he had been there, Jamie had grown to loathe the treacherous land. He had often lain in bed thinking of his nightmare, thinking of all the dreams that people had and wondering where they went to. But the spell in the Land of Perpetual Dreams had cured him of his curiosity. There was a time for being awake and a time for being asleep, he realized, and it was dangerous and fool-hardy to confuse the two. Jamie had always felt somehow cheated when, on waking, a dream that had been so clear and memorable had simply faded away. Now, for the first time, he understood how fortunate it was that those night-time fantasies defied memory.

They belong to the night, he thought, and that is where they should remain. He began counting off the ten minutes that Elizabeth had suggested.

'One, banana skin, two, banana skin, three, banana skin, four, banana skin,' he began chanting.

'What on earth are you doing?' Elizabeth asked, looking at him strangely.

'Counting, banana skin, twelve, banana skin.'

'And the bananas?'

'You have to, banana skin. It helps you, banana skin, to count, banana skin, at just the right, banana skin, speed, banana skin,' he said. 'Twenty-three, banana skin, twenty-four . . .'

'Whatever you say,' said Elizabeth, and while Jamie con-tinued his countdown, she sat down on the podium to wait.

'Fifty-five, banana skin, fifty-six, banana skin, fifty-seven . . .'

—10—
ANOTHER SLEEPLESS NIGHT

At ten past seven, Rory McCrory could ignore the angry clamouring no longer. Children from all over the island had begun assembling outside the hall from five o'clock onwards. Two hours later, when the show was due to commence, there was a noisy crowd of excited youngsters all jostling and jockeying for position, eager to get a good seat when the doors did finally open. Seven came and went and the hall remained locked. A couple of the boys at the front began pounding on the door: a lone voice was soon joined by others, until the air echoed with their demands.

'We want the picture show! We want the picture show! We want the picture show!'

Inside the hall, Alex looked at Fiona nervously.

'Perhaps we ought to let them in,' he said.

'Just a couple of minutes more.'

'You can see why I didn't want to cancel it,' McCrory said. 'They'd have lynched me.'

Fiona nodded. She hadn't liked the idea of going on with

135

the show as if nothing had happened, but she had to concede that *she* wouldn't have liked to tell the increasingly impatient children that the evening's performance was off. On the other hand, as no one knew what might happen if Jamie tried to return while the Traumascope was running, she was anxious to leave it till the last possible moment before opening up.

By quarter past it was clear that they couldn't delay any longer. The panelling in the doors was beginning to rattle ominously under the continuous pummelling of countless little fists.

'I'll tell them there's been a temporary technical hitch,' said McCrory.

He slid the bolts across at the top and bottom, and unlocked the door. If he had hoped to speak rationally to the assembled boys and girls about the unfortunate delay and then reclose the door on them, he was to be disappointed. The moment the children heard the metallic scraping of the first bolt, they all fell silent. As the key turned in the lock, a wild cheer went up and McCrory's attempts to open the door only partially were instantly confounded. With the children at the back surging forward, those at the front burst into the hall, sending the doors crashing back against the walls and McCrory sprawling to the floor.

'Yeeeaaahhh!' the children cheered, as they poured in and raced down the aisles for the seats nearest the screen.

McCrory sat on the floor, smiling. He couldn't help feeling proud of the enthusiasm and loyalty he had instilled in the children. Who cared what his sons and his wife and his erstwhile friends thought about his life on the road? These were the people *Rory McCrory's Travelling Picture Show* was for — and they loved it.

A loud crash from the front of the hall brought him back to the matter at hand. He leapt to his feet. It was immediately clear what had happened.

'Be careful!' he bellowed, and pushed his way through the sea of children.

'I'm . . . I'm sorry,' Alex was saying. 'I just . . . You don't think it's broken, do you?'

'I hope not,' McCrory said gruffly, as he crouched down to inspect the damage.

It hadn't really been Alex's fault. Seeing the pack of grinning, shrieking children racing towards him, it was as if his nightmare had once again come back to taunt and torment him. Instinctively, he had stepped backwards — straight into the screen. Fiona and Dougie Drew had watched the flimsy, top-heavy object teetering on its spindly legs, unable to move, unable to prevent the inevitable. Everything seemed to become impossibly slow as gravity took control and brought the whole lot slamming down on to the floor. The hook which attached the bottom of the screen to the outer frame leapt from its eye, and the spring yanked the roll of silvery canvas back into its protective covering. Those who had seen the accident groaned, and a buzz went round the hall: 'the screen's been smashed'.

'Just straighten this out,' McCrory said as he realigned one of the twisted legs, 'pull this up here, tighten these, and . . . Bob's your uncle.'

He had the contraption standing again. It looked stable enough. Reaching up, he took hold of the ornate handle at the top of the frame and tentatively pulled downwards. All the children held their breath as McCrory slowly unrolled the screen. They knew that if a jagged rip suddenly emerged, the show would be have to be called off. The suspense was intolerable.

A single sigh of relief filled the air as the children saw that no obvious harm had been done to the screen. McCrory was inspecting for any cracks or scratches in the white surface when the leg appeared. This was swiftly followed by an arm, a body and a grinning face. The next moment, Jamie jumped down on to the floor. The boys and girls in the audience went wild, clapping and cheering at the unbelievable trick they had just witnessed.

'Jamie!' Fiona and Alex yelled.

'Hiya,' he said, and tugged at the hand he was holding. 'Come on, don't be shy.'

It was only then that the others realized a second arm was coming through the screen. McCrory gasped as he recognized the deep-red hair and freckly white skin.

'Elizabeth,' he said.

She jumped down beside Jamie and another round of applause exploded from the captivated audience. Elizabeth seemed not to notice where she was. She looked at McCrory.

'You've aged,' she said.

'I dare say I have.'

'All those little grey bits in your beard — and the wrinkles round your eyes. You smile too much.'

McCrory wasn't smiling now. He stared at Elizabeth, the little girl who had disappeared all those years ago. He thought he'd never see her again. All the questions he'd wanted to ask her for so long had deserted him. He was speechless.

'You haven't changed at all,' he finally managed to say.

'Oh, I have, I have,' Elizabeth said. 'I might not *look* like a middle-aged housewife . . .'

'Why didn't you come back?'

'I couldn't,' she said simply. 'It wasn't time.'

'But . . .'

'It took Jamie here to show me that sometimes you have to let go of your dreams.'

'Especially when they're nightmares,' Jamie chipped in.

'But twenty years,' McCrory said.

'Dreams don't follow the rules of time,' Elizabeth explained. 'Twenty years is like a day, while a minute can sometimes take for ever.'

Having come to the conclusion that the magic show was over and no more people were going to appear out of nowhere, the boys and girls were beginning to get restless once again. Some of those at the back began whistling and flicking popcorn. A slow and sonorous handclap started up.

'We'll talk later,' McCrory said hurriedly. 'I can't keep this lot waiting a moment longer.'

'That's all right,' said Jamie. 'I'll show Elizabeth some of what she's missed over the last twenty years.'

'You're welcome to stay and watch the show,' McCrory said.

Elizabeth smiled wryly. 'If it's all the same to you, I'll give it a miss.'

'Of course, of course,' McCrory said, striding back up the aisle towards the Traumascope.

'Come on,' said Alex, 'there's a side-door over here.'

'Don't *you* want to stay either?' Jamie asked.

'No, thank you,' he and Fiona said in unison. Their own nightmares were still far too fresh in their memory for them to tempt fate by remaining, now that the Traumascope had been switched on again.

'Once was quite enough,' said Fiona.

'You mean, you . . . ?'

'I'll tell you everything once we're outside,' she said. 'And get a move on, it's about to start.'

Even as she was speaking, the hall-lights went out and the dazzling light of the Traumascope cut through the darkness. The silhouette of four startled figures was outlined against the screen. A moment later they had disappeared, racing off towards the side-door before the curious beam could once again start probing into the hidden recesses of their minds.

*

By the time the show came to an end, Elizabeth had sampled frozen yoghurt and dry-roasted peanuts, listened to the latest Number One album on a CD personal stereo, watched herself on video — courtesy of one of the more modern inventions in Rory McCrory's collection — and discovered that life was, despite technological advances, much the same as when she had left it twenty years before. She and Jamie described their experiences in the Land of Perpetual Dreams and, not to be outdone, Alex and Fiona told them of the horrors *they'd* had to endure when the Traumascope had run amok.

'All I hope,' Jamie said, 'is that my parents don't mess things up.'

'Do you really think they'll let Elizabeth stay?' Alex said.

'I can't imagine what she'll do if they refuse,' Fiona said.

'Hey,' said Elizabeth, 'is talking about someone as if she wasn't there another new craze?'

'Sorry,' said Alex, reddening. 'It's just that . . .' Under Fiona's forbidding gaze, he fell silent, realizing that he should keep his misgivings about Mr MacDonald to himself.

'I don't care if they don't want me,' Elizabeth said defiantly. 'I'll go somewhere else.'

'You could travel with me,' McCrory said, appearing at the door with the Traumascope, reels and screen.

Elizabeth looked at him and laughed. 'Oh, please, Jamie, please make your father say yes. Anything but a life on the road with Rory McCrory!'

'How was the show?' Fiona asked. 'No one disappeared, I trust.'

The others sniggered.

'Not as far as I know,' said McCrory stiffly. 'Now who's going to give me a hand with the packing up?'

Now that they were all reunited, everyone was keen to get back to Skye as quickly as possible, and it didn't take long to get the caravan ready. The shutters were secured, the generator chugged into action and, with Major in place between the wooden shafts, McCrory organized the seating.

'Alex, Fiona,' he said, 'if you'd like to ride up at the front with Dougie, then I can go in the caravan with Jamie and Elizabeth. Is that all right?'

'Fine,' said Fiona, leaping up on to the padded bench.

'And it's OK with you, is it?' McCrory asked Elizabeth gently.

She nodded. 'I'd like to talk.'

The caravan jolted off over the cobblestones as Major trundled back down to the harbour. Inside the warm, plush interior of the caravan, McCrory gave Jamie and Elizabeth a Cola each, while he opened a bottle of red wine for himself.

'At least this hasn't changed,' Elizabeth said, raising her can. 'Not that I got to drink it particularly often. Great-Aunt Grizelda wouldn't allow it in the house. Said you might just as well drink rat poison. I remember I had it once at a church bazaar. Aunt Thomasina was furious,' she grinned, 'but as the vicar had given it to me, she couldn't very well cause a fuss.'

McCrory smiled. 'So that was it?' he said. 'You didn't have any reason to return.'

'My whole life was a nightmare,' she said. 'There was nothing in the Land of Perputual Dreams that scared me half as much.'

'Except for your own one,' said Jamie quietly.

'Except for that,' Elizabeth admitted. 'But I only saw it once – well, once and a half if you count our trip,' she said to Jamie.

'So . . . I mean . . .' McCrory was finding it difficult to say what he wanted.

And Elizabeth wasn't making it any easier for him. She stared at him calmly, waiting for him to come out with his question. Like Jamie, McCrory realized that Elizabeth's years in the curious land had given her a deep insight into people's minds. As she continued to look into his eyes, he had the feeling that she could read his mind.

'I'll leave it up to you,' McCrory said, trying a new tack. 'It can be your decision – I know what your friend thinks about the matter,' he added, looking at Jamie.

'What?' said Jamie. He hadn't a clue what McCrory was going on about.

'Fiona thinks it's irresponsible of me to keep on with the picture show. She blamed me for your disappearance,' he said to Jamie. 'Claimed I had no business using the Traumascope when I knew how dangerous it could be – when I knew that someone had already . . . But you're back again now, Elizabeth.'

'Better late than never, as Jamie so wisely observed,' she said, and the pair of them laughed.

Jamie realized how far away the world on the other side of the screen now was. Like a nightmare itself, which fades away to nothing when you wake, the memory of the Land of Perpetual Dreams was already blurred. McCrory was becoming increasingly agitated.

'Well?' he said. 'What do you think? Should I keep the show on the road and continue healing nightmares, or is the Traumascope simply too hazardous to expose young minds to? Should I or shouldn't I carry on?'

Elizabeth looked at Rory McCrory as though he were an idiot.

'But, of course you carry on,' she said incredulously.

'I do?' he said, genuinely surprised.

'Naturally. The good you've done far outweighs the couple of mishaps that have occurred – and even they weren't too bad, were they?' she said to Jamie. He shook his head.

She even talks like a grown-up, McCrory thought. Half the time he wasn't a hundred per cent sure what she was talking about. The fact that she thought he should continue with his Real-to-Reel Picture Show was clear enough, however. And Jamie agreed.

'It's only kids with *really* disturbing memories who get sucked into the screen to confront their own nightmares,' he explained.

'And it saves them being scarred for life,' said Elizabeth. 'No, you definitely can't stop now — in fact, seeing as you're not getting any younger, perhaps you ought to be training up a replacement.'

'Cheeky so-and-so,' McCrory grinned.

'How old *are* you?' Jamie asked.

'As old as my eyes, as old as my nose, and a little bit older than my teeth,' McCrory answered cryptically.

'No, really,' said Jamie.

But Rory McCrory wasn't giving anything away, and the sounds and smells of the harbour put paid to any further questions. The caravan jolted to a halt.

'Right,' McCrory said. 'Let's load up the boat.'

Happy now that he had been given the go-ahead by the one person he thought might hate him for what had happened, McCrory was pottering about, whistling something loud and tuneless. It was dark outside and the harbour lights were reflected unbroken in the calm water. Overhead, the stars were twinkling brightly.

'You're sure you don't mind about the crossing?' Fiona asked Jamie.

'Why should I?'

'Well, the water . . .'

'What of it?'

Fiona looked at her friend curiously. Had he forgotten how terrified of the sea he was? She decided not to pursue the matter. But if she had thought Jamie was merely putting on a brave face in front of Elizabeth and McCrory, she was soon to be proved wrong. Before the others had realized what he was doing, Jamie had pulled off his shoes and socks, shorts and jumper, and was wading into the still water in his underpants.

'Jamie, what on earth are you doing?' she said.

'You'll catch your death,' Elizabeth said.

'Shuddup, Mum,' he said, and continued in, right up to his waist. Then, raising his hands above his head, he dived in and swam underwater breaststroke until he was out of his depth. Then he stopped, resurfaced and, treading water, waved back at the anxious onlookers.

'Come on in,' he yelled, 'the water's lovely.'

Seeing that the boy was in no trouble, despite his friends' obvious concern, McCrory pulled his boots back on. A rescue attempt would not be necessary.

'We ought to be making tracks while the tide's in,' he said. 'Alex, go and fetch Jamie a towel from the caravan.'

Jamie was happy to return to the shore. He had proved that he'd overcome the fear of water which had paralysed him so often in the past. His nightmare had offered him the key to solving his problem, and he had turned it willingly. Never again would he be frightened of a swimming-pool, a river — or even the sea. He swam back to the beach with strong overarm strokes and confident kicking feet.

'Wonderful,' he said, as he took the towel and began rubbing himself down.

Fiona looked at him. He was violently trembling, but on this occasion it was not with the blind terror she had seen so many times before, but merely the cold. Even sceptical, down-to-earth Fiona was now convinced that the show would have to carry on. She caught McCrory's eye and smiled.

'Ready?' he asked everyone.

'Ready,' came the reply.

Spirits were high as the *Ben-Davy* chugged out of the harbour and, as the lights of Lochmaddy faded into the distance, they were replaced by the glow of the rising crescent moon. It was one o'clock in the morning on their second night without sleep, but although everyone felt giddy and lightheaded, nobody wanted to go to bed. The water was as calm as a millpond and the four children peered down at the silver line which ran directly from the moon to the boat.

'It's as if we're not moving,' Alex said, as the light continued to follow them.

'Reminds me of a nightmare I once saw,' said Elizabeth. 'There was this boat crossing the sea, and all of a sudden it was surrounded by a stinking mass of fluorescent algae that swallowed . . .'

'We don't want to hear!' the others yelled immediately.

'All right, all right. Keep your hair on,' Elizabeth grinned.

Having finished his wine, McCrory went through the ritual of writing the message on the card and sealing it inside the bottle.

'It'll change your life, eh?' said Elizabeth.

'You mean, you read the message too?' said Fiona.

'I didn't realize I'd been doing it so long,' said McCrory. 'I wonder just how many bottles I've chucked into the sea around Britain over the years.'

'You drink too much,' said Jamie seriously. He couldn't help thinking of Moira and what the whisky had done to her.

'Hey,' McCrory said in mock anger. 'That's no way to talk to your elders and betters.'

'Betters?' Fiona shrieked.

'Well, elders, anyway,' said McCrory.

'Not even so sure about that,' Dougie Drew called over from the wheel, 'the way you were thrashing around at the sofa with that wet towel. Looked a right idiot, you did.'

Jamie's comment had been defused by the laughter, but he stuck by what he'd said. He didn't like the way alcohol made people so unpredictable. One minute they'd be all giggly and silly; the next, they'd fly into an illogical rage over nothing at all. It made him feel ill-at-ease.

He looked down into the deep water and watched the v-shaped ripple opening up behind him. And as he stared, the face of his sister appeared for a moment. Her brown hair hung over her bony shoulders, her blue eyes twinkled. She was smiling. Here was the Moira he remembered: the kind and caring older sister, who had shielded him from everything unpleasant. And he realized that this memory was just as real as the rebellious version he had also seen. Now that he was nearly as old as she had been when she'd died, he felt he understood her so much better. She could be nice and nasty, sympathetic and spiteful, generous to a fault and totally self-centred. His idealized memory hadn't been of a real person at all. It was as Elizabeth had said: Moira was just a typical teenager. And he missed her. The smiling face in the waves began to fade.

'Are you all right?' a voice asked.

Jamie turned round. It was Elizabeth.

'I don't want to replace her,' she said, 'no one ever could.'

'I know,' said Jamie. 'Everything's fine. Really!'

The sky was tinged with pale blue streaks of morning as the *Ben-Davy* entered the loch. In the distance, the six passengers watched the street-lamps switching off, one by one, as they approached Portree. All of them were exhausted, all of them were relieved to be back.

'Look,' said Alex, 'policemen.'

He was right. Among the crowd of people waiting on the jetty for the boat's arrival were three men in dark uniforms, waiting to question the returning wanderers.

'But how did they know?' Fiona asked.

'I radioed ahead after last night's show,' McCrory said. 'I thought it would be best.'

As they drew nearer, it became clear that the message had got round. Jamie's disappearance and Alex and Fiona's attempts to find him were no longer a private matter. The incident had become public property, and the three of them spent the last few minutes picking out the assortment of individuals who had turned up to greet their arrival.

Apart from the policemen, there were Mr and Mrs Mac-Donald, Mr and Mrs McKintosh – Alex and Fiona's parents – Liam Donahue, the boy whose chainsaw nightmare had been cured, and his cousin John Girvan. Various other friends and neighbours stood round in twos and threes, guessing and gossiping, each with their own theory of what had happened. To the right was a group of fishermen, wondering what had caused everyone to get up so unusually early: on a typical morning, they would have the entire harbour to themselves.

Having steered into a vacant berth, Dougie Drew secured the ropes to the steel rings of the jetty wall. None of the onlookers made a move.

'Into the lions' den, I suppose,' said McCrory.

'They're not going to arrest you, are they?' Fiona said. 'You haven't done anything.'

'As you yourself said, Fiona, strictly speaking I abducted you.'

'I said *kidnapped*,' she said. 'But that was before I knew that –'

'Save it for the boys in blue,' said McCrory.

'Well, I'll stand up for you,' said Jamie.

McCrory smiled bashfully. 'I want you all to know,' he said, looking at each of the children in turn, 'that whatever happens, I'll never forget any of you. In my thirty years or so on the road, I have never had such a wonderful couple of

147

days. Fiona, Alex, you impressed me so much with your loyalty and perseverance – I'm grateful to you for making me question the Traumascope and the travelling picture show. For questioning myself. I had become too arrogant.'

The pair of them blushed. Fiona, in particular, felt distinctly uneasy when she thought of all the accusations she had levelled against the man.

'And Jamie,' McCrory continued. 'Well, what can I say? You must have gone through so much in the Land of Perpetual Dreams. Hopefully, it wasn't *too* painful. And then you found Elizabeth ... I can't even begin to thank you enough for bringing Elizabeth back safely.'

It was Jamie's turn to look away, his face red with embarrassment at the praise being heaped upon him.

'And as for you,' McCrory said to Elizabeth herself. 'You can't imagine the nightmares I've had about what might have happened to you. All those years.'

'I'm back now,' she said simply.

'Yes,' said McCrory. 'I don't know what the authorities are going to say. They might even destroy the Traumascope, I suppose. But it means so much knowing that you, of all people, would like to see the picture show continue.'

There was silence. Everyone felt slightly uncomfortable at McCrory's show of emotion.

'Oi,' came a voice from the back. 'Haven't you forgotten someone?' It was Dougie Drew. He had noticed how near to tears McCrory was, and to save his old friend the ignominy of sobbing in front of the children, he drew their attention away.

'Who?' said McCrory.

'Me!' he exclaimed. 'All very well thanking any old Tom, Dick and Harry like that, but if it wasn't for me, it wouldn't be a travelling show at all. Rory McCrory's Real-to-Reel *Stationary* Picture Show. Can't see that drawing in the crowds, can you? Hasn't got the same ring.'

'And last but not least,' McCrory said theatrically, relieved that the moment of emotion had passed. 'To Dougie Drew; my heartiest appreciation, my sincerest gratitude and unconditional thanks. Thanks a lot, skipper!'

Dougie Drew acknowledged McCrory's words with a regal wave of his hand and a low, elegant bow.

'And now,' McCrory proclaimed.

> *'The time has come to step ashore,*
> *To face the music and settle the score,*
> *And if I'm sent to a prison cell*
> *Think of me and wish me well.*

'No, they couldn't, we won't let them, they wouldn't dare,' came the immediate chatter of raised voices.

McCrory looked at the four indignant faces and grinned. 'Just joshing,' he said.

But Alex and Fiona, Jamie and Elizabeth, all noticed how quickly the smile vanished as he turned away. Rory Mc-Crory was a worried man — though not half as worried as Jamie. While McCrory introduced himself to the police, and Alex and Fiona bounded over towards their parents, Jamie held back. He shuffled about awkwardly and fiddled with a length of string in the right-hand pocket of his shorts.

All the people who had gathered on the jetty to greet the arrival of the boat were milling about, piecing together the children's escapade bit by bit. All the people, that is, except for Mr and Mrs MacDonald. Jamie looked up and observed them carefully. His mother seemed as withdrawn as always. Her hair was uncombed and there were dark circles under her eyes; a calico bag lay at her feet.

Probably spent the entire night knitting, thought Jamie, smiling inwardly.

He glanced at his father. The man looked sterner than he had ever seen him before. His thin lips were pressed so tightly together that they had formed a narrow line, resembling a scar more than a mouth. And his eyebrows — always dark and threatening — were now drawn together into one menacing, black band low over the glaring eyes. Jamie looked around him nervously. Whatever he might have said to Elizabeth, he had loved his days away from home. It wouldn't have taken much for him to turn tail and run. The trouble was, there was nowhere to run to. Standing at the end of the jetty, he had no option but to walk ahead and face his parents.

With his eyes fixed to the ground, he advanced towards them. Now that the excitement was over, his whole body felt immensely weary. Jamie hadn't realized how long the jetty was. He stopped. As if reluctant to carry the boy on towards the inevitable confrontation, his leaden legs had refused to take him a step further. Jamie raised his head and was immediately trapped by his father's steely gaze. He tried in vain to turn his head and look away. It was hopeless. His father had all but mesmerized the tired boy and he remained rooted to the spot, staring at his opponent like a cowboy in a high-noon shoot-out.

It was Mr MacDonald who made the first move. He walked stiffly towards his son, Mrs MacDonald in tow. As he approached, Jamie was forced to tilt his head slowly upwards until, with the man towering above him, he found himself staring directly into the bright, rising sun. His father's head was silhouetted against it, black and featureless.

I wonder if he's going to hit me? Jamie thought.

But Mr MacDonald was not a violent man. Although he had hurt Jamie too often in the past, it had been with sarcasm and rage, never with his hands. And at that particular moment, nothing could have been further from Mr MacDonald's mind than striking his son.

He saw in the frightened eyes and trembling lower lip, the three-year-old he should have cuddled and comforted all those years ago. He would not make the same mistake twice. Without speaking, he crouched down in front of his son and opened his arms to him. Jamie saw tears welling up in his eyes.

The hug was the biggest, warmest, wonderfullest hug in the whole world. And it went on for ages and ages. Too long, in fact: Jamie began to get itchy with self-consciousness, knowing that Liam and John were probably watching. But his father showed no sign of letting go. This was the hug of a lifetime, to try and make up for all the occasions he'd treated Jamie coldly. It was a hug that said sorry; that said please forgive me and let's start all over. Jamie realized that his father was crying. His body was heaving and loud sobs were gulping into Jamie's ear. He opened his eyes and looked up at his mother. Tears were streaming down her cheeks too.

'Oh, Jamie, Jamie, Jamie,' she sniffed. 'We thought we'd lost you like . . . like . . .'

Mr MacDonald pulled away from his son and, holding him by his arms, looked into his eyes.

'Like Moira,' he said.

Jamie stared back. It was the first time he had heard her name mentioned since she had died.

'You see, when you were a little boy . . .' his father began.

'Three years old,' his mother added.

'We were having a picnic and she . . . and she . . .' The tears welled up again.

'I know,' said Jamie. He couldn't let them punish themselves any longer. 'It's all right.'

His mother leant down, stroked his cheek and kissed him on the forehead.

'We love you so much,' she said.

'It's all right,' Jamie repeated, as his embarrassment began to surface again.

'I'll make it up to you,' Mr MacDonald said, and smiled awkwardly. 'You see if I don't.'

Jamie saw the opportunity he'd been waiting for. He glanced round. Elizabeth was standing a couple of steps back, watching the family reunion. Her pale face betrayed nothing of what she was thinking, but Jamie thought he could guess. He smiled.

'Mum, Dad,' he said, pulling away from his father. 'There's someone I want you to meet.' He took a deep breath: 'This is Elizabeth.'

EPILOGUE

'Where on earth is it?' Jamie said, going through his cupboard for the third time. 'It must be here somewhere.'

He decided to be more scientific about the search and instead of rummaging through the packed shelves, began pulling everything out piece by piece. It was amazing how much junk you could accumulate. Everything but the kitchen sink! But no torch. The last time he'd used it was on Firework Night, and he was positive he'd put it back afterwards. So where was it? There could be only one explanation and, having shoved everything back into the cupboard and irritably slammed the doors shut, he stomped off to the bedroom opposite.

It looked different now. The dolls, teddies and fluffy animals had all been consigned to a box in the attic, as had the posters of Boy George and the Police. Elizabeth's taste was quite different. She'd Blu-tacked watercolour sketches she'd painted above her bed, there were dried flowers in a vase near the window and bowls of pot-pourri on the window-ledge. She'd bought several books too and the shelves were full of all the authors she'd missed over the previous twenty years.

'Have you had my torch again?' he demanded.

Elizabeth pointed to the chest-of-drawers. 'Sorry,' she said, 'I needed it the other day.'

'You could have asked.'

'I said I was sorry.'

'Well, why can't you put things back? I thought I'd lost it.'

'So-rry,' Elizabeth repeated impatiently. 'Anyway, I can't find my Walkman. You wouldn't happen to know where that might be . . . ?'

'I borrowed it last night,' he mumbled.

'You could have asked!' Elizabeth said, mimicking his own impatience.

Jamie looked away angrily. She always had to get the last word. In many ways, it'd been more difficult for Jamie to adjust to someone else living in the house than for his parents. He was used to being alone; he was used to things remaining where he left them. Elizabeth grinned at him.

'Don't be such a grump,' she said. 'Look at you!'

Jamie glanced in the mirror. The knitted brow and pouting mouth were not a pretty sight, he had to admit.

'Well!' he said, but smirked despite himself.

'Hurry up, you two,' Mr MacDonald called down the corridor.

'Coming,' said Jamie, grabbed the torch and rushed back to his own room to finish packing.

Taking everything into account, Elizabeth's moving in had worked out very well. The disadvantage of the occasional 'borrowed' object was more than outweighed by the advantages of having another young person in the house. The atmosphere was different now. Everyone talked more, sang more, laughed and joked more. In short, Elizabeth had brought 18 Dougall Street back to life.

Of course, Jamie hadn't known things would go so smoothly. That morning on the jetty six months ago, when he'd finally plucked up courage to ask if she could stay, he'd been sure his parents would say no. The quick look they'd given one another had seemed to confirm it.

'But what about Elizabeth's parents?' Mrs MacDonald had asked.

Jamie explained, as best he could, all about the picture show and the Traumascope and the nightmares that had pulled both him and Elizabeth into the screen.

'Mm-hmm,' said Mr MacDonald, rolling his eyes. Jamie recognized the signs of mounting impatience. Any second now he'd say something that everyone would regret. Mrs MacDonald intervened.

'Elizabeth,' she said, 'we'll have to check on a couple of the details — you must admit, it's a pretty hard story to swallow — but if . . . I mean, as long as . . .' She smiled; 'we'd love you to come and stay.'

It was a wet Wednesday during half-term, and Jamie and Elizabeth were playing whist when the information finally arrived. It was confirmed that an Elizabeth McNulty, ward of Misses G. and T. Taylor, had disappeared in 1971. Grizelda Taylor had died two years later at the age of 105. Her daughter, Thomasina, followed her to the grave a week after that.

None of it made any sense to Mrs MacDonald, but then neither had the rumours that had been circulating the island about McCrory and his travelling picture show. At any rate, Elizabeth was neither a runaway nor a criminal, and in the three weeks since she'd arrived, Mrs MacDonald had grown to like the curiously old-fashioned girl. She was welcome to live with them as long as she liked.

'Will you get a move on!' shouted Mr MacDonald.

Jamie zipped up his bag, grabbed it by the handles and raced towards the door. Before getting there, however, he skidded to a halt. There was something that he'd forgotten, propped up against the light on his bedside table.

It was when they had been shifting the cardboard boxes full of Moira's belongings up to the loft that Jamie had found the photograph. It was one of a whole wad which had been stuffed into a biscuit tin and hidden from sight. After their daughter's death, both Mr and Mrs MacDonald had found it intolerable to be reminded of the family of four they had once been. As Jamie held the picture up, his hand had begun to tremble. The four faces grinning into the camera, blissfully ignorant of the tragedy awaiting them.

'Can I have it?' Jamie had asked his parents.

'Of course you can,' said Mr MacDonald. 'Just look at how happy we all were,' he smiled. 'Life can be so cruel.'

Jamie didn't mention the bad feelings between father and daughter that had soured the afternoon picnic, nor did he remind him that it was his own confusion with the words flash and flasher that had triggered off the happy smiles. Mr MacDonald was entitled to keep his memories intact, no matter how idealized they might be.

From that day on, Jamie kept the photograph next to his bed. He would look at it last thing at night and first thing in the morning. Now that they were going away, he decided to take it with him. He slipped it into the middle of his exercise book — full now of far more interesting diary entries than the comings and goings of the neighbour's dog — and pushed the book into his inside pocket. He was ready.

'At long last,' his exasperated father said, when Jamie finally appeared in the sitting-room.

'Sorry, I . . .' Jamie began.

'I don't want to know,' Mr MacDonald interrupted. 'We're late enough as it is.'

Jamie and Elizabeth grinned at one another and followed Mr MacDonald out to the car. When he'd announced that he was planning to take a long weekend off and suggested that they all get away for a few days, he'd expected that the kids would want to go to the mainland: Edinburgh or Dundee perhaps, or if they'd really set their heart on a walk, Ben Nevis. But no, they'd been insistent. He'd tried in vain to dissuade them, but the Cuillin Mountains it had to be.

Baffled, but eager to do what they wanted, Mr Mac-Donald had consented. He didn't realize the significance of the place. He couldn't know that for Jamie and Elizabeth, the treacherous, disorientating mountains were their link to all they had learnt in the Land of Perpetual Dreams.

And what of Rory McCrory himself? Well, as no one seemed willing to press charges, the police had no alternative but to let him go. He celebrated his freedom with an evening in the pub, which had turned into a two-month drinking binge. The entire episode had upset McCrory far more than he had acknowledged and, despite the assurances from Elizabeth and Jamie that he should continue with the show, he remained unconvinced. The responsibility for the welfare of his young audiences was too great – he thought he would not be able to live with himself if another child disappeared. Two separate incidents were to convince him otherwise.

McCrory had parked his caravan in the car-park of the White Thistle – it was handy for the bar and the landlord had invited him to eat with the family. Having breakfast one morning, he noticed how awful the man's youngest son looked. The dark bags under his eyes made his pale skin look all the more sickly.

'It's the nightmares,' the landlord said quietly. 'Same one every night, isn't it, Oliver?'

The boy merely nodded.

'The doctor says it's just a phase he's going through, but . . . I just feel so useless.'

McCrory remained silent. He didn't dare to offer his services. True, the Traumascope might cure the boy of his night-time torment, but what if his nightmares were so bad that he too was sucked through the screen? How would the landlord react then?

'Oh, I nearly forgot. This arrived for you earlier,' he added, handing him an envelope.

McCrory looked at the front. The postmark confirmed that it had taken nearly three weeks to reach him, having been half way round the Hebrides already. That it had arrived at all was a minor miracle in itself, he realized when reading the scrawled post office messages on the back. *Not known at this address — try Coll. Try Tiree. Try Harris. NO NOT HERE EITHER — LEWIS?* And it was here, on the Outer Hebridean island of Lewis, that the letter had finally caught up with him.

'It had better be worth all the trouble,' McCrory said, licking the marmalade off his knife and slitting the envelope open. He pulled out the single piece of writing paper and glanced immediately at the back to see who it was from. Jamie and Elizabeth, he read.

What on earth can they want? he wondered, and skimmed quickly through the letter for any mention that the police might wish to reopen the case. He needn't have worried. Far from bringing bad news, their letter made him feel better than he had in weeks.

> *Dear Rory McCrory,*
>
> *We wanted to thank you in person for all you did for us, but you left before we had a chance, so a letter will have to do. I've settled in at the MacDonalds' very well. They're really nice when you get to know them.*
>
> *If it hadn't been for you, I don't know what either of us*

would have done. We're both so grateful. If you were ever in any doubt about continuing with the picture show, then I hope you've seen sense. What you offer kids is far too valuable for you to stop.

Elizabeth had signed the letter and Jamie had added his own name and the PS — *'I'll be fourteen in just over a year, so don't leave it too long before your next trip to Skye!'*

McCrory had smiled as he folded the letter up and slipped it back into the envelope. He remembered the way the two curiously earnest faces had looked at him, and knew they wouldn't approve of what he was doing now. You drink too much, Jamie had said. It was true. Ever since he had left the police station, he had been wallowing in self-pity, and the alcohol was only making things worse.

'Good news, I hope,' the landlord said.

McCrory nodded. 'The best,' he said. 'And you know what? I can't promise anything, of course, but I might be able to help young Oliver.'

The coincidence had stirred McCrory from his uncertainty and depression. Omens like that couldn't be denied, and he decided there and then that he *would* take the show back on the road.

The picture show is still travelling round the coast and islands of Great Britain, and McCrory's Traumascope has helped to cure countless boys and girls of their worst nightmares. So far — touch wood — no one else has been dragged into the Land of Perpetual Dreams, but McCrory was happy in the knowledge that, even if it should happen again, everything would turn out for the best.

If you don't happen to see his posters advertising the show but need to go to a performance, then scour the beach for washed-up bottles. You might be lucky. One of them might contain the personal invitation from Rory McCrory himself.

But don't bother with wine bottles, if you find any. Ever since that Saturday morning when he made his decision to continue, not a drop of alcohol has passed his lips. These days his rolled-up messages are to be found in lemonade and Cola bottles.

Be careful though! If you should come across one of Rory McCrory's handwritten invitations, think twice before you accept. A visit to *Rory McCrory's Real-to-Reel Picture Show* should not be taken lightly.

After all, as Jamie MacDonald and Elizabeth McNulty know only too well, it'll change your life!